"So are you?" Gloria asks. "Are you going to win?"

I shrug my shoulders.

"The winner gets a check for two thousand dollars. And a trophy almost as tall as a man," Gloria explains to a few other girls standing around.

"Two thousand dollars!" Alicia Weber says, dropping her jaw.

Again, I shrug. The money would be nice. And the trophy, too. But it really isn't why I'm a giant pumpkin grower.

Me and the Pumpkin Queen

by Marlane Kennedy

Greenwillow Books
An Imprint of HarperCollinsPublishers

Me and the Pumpkin Queen
Text copyright © 2007 by Marlane Kennedy

The text of this book is set in Caslon.
Book design by Victoria Jamieson

Library of Congress Cataloging-in-Publication Data
Kennedy, Marlane.
Me and the pumpkin queen / by Marlane Kennedy.
p. cm.
"Greenwillow Books"
Summary: Although Aunt Arlene tries to interest her in clothing and growing up, ten-year-old Mildred is entirely focused on growing a pumpkin big enough to win the annual Circleville, Ohio, contest, as her mother dreamed of doing before she died.
ISBN: 978-0-06-114022-8 (trade bdg.)
ISBN: 978-0-06-114023-5 (lib. bdg.)
ISBN: 978-0-06-114024-2 (pbk.)
[1. Pumpkin—Fiction. 2. Gardening—Fiction. 3. Aunts—Fiction.
4. Single-parent families—Fiction. 5. Grief—Fiction.] I. Title.
PZ7.K3846Me 2007 [Fic]—dc22 2006020019

09 10 11 12 13 CG/CW 10 9 8 7 6 5 4 3 2 1

First HarperTrophy edition, 2009

In memory of Molly and for my husband, Joel,
and our children, Seth, Spencer, and Hope

For my parents, Marvin and Laney Stulley, my sister,
Marsha Waidelich, and my brother, Mark Stulley

And for the good people of Circleville, whose passion
for anything pumpkin, come the third Wednesday of October,
is truly a sight to behold

Me and the Pumpkin Queen

Chapter 1

I don't think I'm abnormally obsessive. I mean, Daddy hasn't taken me to the doctor or anything to find out for sure, so I prefer to describe myself as focused. A lot of kids my age are focused. Like Arnie Bradford. He is focused on basketball. Every time we drive by his house on our way to town, he is in his driveway shooting baskets. Even in the middle of winter. Then there is Gloria Mathis. She is all the time blathering about this teenage actor she is in love with. She cuts his picture out of magazines and plasters them all over her school notebooks.

But truth be told, they are focused on the usual kinds of things that kids all over the place are focused on. Like there are probably hundreds of thousands of fifth graders into basketball and popular actors. It just so happens that my thoughts are consumed with something out of the ordinary. Daddy isn't worried about me at all. But Aunt Arlene sure is.

Chapter 2

Maybe Daddy isn't worried about me because he is kind of focused himself. He is a veterinarian here in Pickaway County, and he keeps real busy. He has an office built into the side of our home, an old white farmhouse with a green tin roof. He is a mixed-animal vet. That means besides the dogs and cats he tends to in our home, he sometimes has to travel to neighboring farms to look after cattle, sheep, pigs, and horses.

We aren't rich. Aunt Arlene says Daddy treats too many animals at a discount and takes on too many pets his clients abandon. But the two of us, we don't care. I don't need to live in a huge house with Persian rugs and stuffy antiques like Aunt Arlene does. I've told her that before, but it's like she can't hear a word that I say.

Aunt Arlene is very focused too. Focused on other people's business. Since we lost Mama, she thinks it is her job to take care of Daddy and me even though we do fine on our own. But she means well, and we love her despite her meddling ways. And I know she loves the two of us despite our obvious flaws, so it all evens out, I suppose, in the end.

And speak of the devil, she is just now interrupting my Saturday morning, the screen door of Daddy's office banging behind her.

Chapter 3

"**I**'m taking the girl shopping for some spring clothes today," Aunt Arlene announces. She doesn't even say hi or greet us in any other way. But we are used to that. She usually announces something upon her arrival.

Daddy is at the front counter with Shirley, his assistant. They are getting things ready for his first scheduled patient of the day, an Old English sheepdog that is being brought in for neutering.

I'm goofing around on the office computer nearby. I click off the message board on

BigPumpkins.com and sigh. I'm not pleased with Aunt Arlene's shopping news. I like spending my Saturday mornings helping around the office. I feed the animals that have had to spend the night, and sometimes answer the phone or greet people. My friend Jacob will probably be stopping by this afternoon, too. Lately he's been trying to teach me how to play chess. He'll be disappointed if I'm not here. Besides, I have no interest in clothes. Daddy just takes me to the discount store, and I get regular jeans and T-shirts. Our shopping trips take all of about fifteen minutes. I have an uneasy feeling, though, that this trip will be an all-day affair.

Daddy looks at me. "You want to go shopping with your aunt Arlene?"

"No."

"The girl doesn't want to go," he says.

I'm often referred to as *the girl* when Daddy and Aunt Arlene discuss me. I'm not offended. After all, I am an only child and therefore the only girl in the family, so there is never any confusion about who they are talking about. Besides, I kind of like being called *the girl*. It is much better than my real name, which happens to be Mildred. I am named after Daddy and Aunt Arlene's mother, my grandma, who now lives in Florida with my grandpa. They moved there when I was three because they couldn't stand the winter weather here in Ohio, but they do visit us for a few weeks every summer. The name suits my grandma just fine; she has wrinkles and smells of old- lady perfume. It just doesn't happen to fit me. A few people have tried to shorten my name to Millie, but it never caught on. It doesn't seem to fit either. Millie sounds perky, and I guess I'm more on the serious side.

Aunt Arlene walks over to Daddy, leans over the counter, and whispers, "The girl is starting to . . . grow. I think it's best that I take her shopping, if you know what I mean."

Daddy seldom blushes, but his face is turning pink. Before he says a word, I know I'm a goner. I'm going shopping with Aunt Arlene.

Chapter 4

Aunt Arlene and I drive by Arnie Bradford's house. He's in the driveway, pounding an orange ball onto blacktop. Aunt Arlene toots her horn and waves.

"Nice boy," she says. "And cute, don't you think?"

I stare at her with an appropriately disgusted look, and she becomes silent.

Just looking at Aunt Arlene, you would never guess she and Daddy are sister and brother. Aunt Arlene is always color-coordinated, with every hair in place. Right now she's wearing khaki pants and a cream blouse with a brown, tan, and blue scarf draped at her neck. She has smooth, chin-length dark brown hair that curls under on the ends.

Daddy's hair is the same color, but it always looks like he just got out of bed; he's not one to blow-dry and gel. And sometimes Aunt Arlene studies what he's wearing and jokes about his being color-blind, which he's not.

I'm a lot like Daddy, although right now my hair doesn't look too bad. Aunt Arlene made me brush it before we left.

I look out the window and think more important thoughts. Pretty soon, as we continue on our way to Aunt Arlene's favorite mall in Columbus, we pass Circleville's water tower. It's painted like a giant pumpkin. But I was thinking about giant pumpkins before it even appeared out my car window. Giant pumpkins are what I'm focused on. Morning, noon, and night I've got giant pumpkins on my mind.

Chapter 5

It all started when I was six. Like always, I had spent part of the third week of October at the Circleville Pumpkin Show, otherwise known as the "Greatest Free Show on Earth" (and I'm not exaggerating about the title; anyone who goes to pumpkinshow.com can print out a ticket that says so).

The streets are blocked off, and more than four hundred thousand people flock to our town. It's such a big deal that all the local schools get three whole days off, even though it's not exactly considered a national holiday.

We have a huge midway, and more rides and junk-food stands than practically any old fair you've been to. And when it comes to food, people don't just fill up on things like cotton candy and caramel apples. We have pumpkin ice cream, pumpkin donuts, pumpkin chili, pumpkin hamburgers, pumpkin pizza, and spaghetti with pumpkin sauce. If it can be made out of pumpkin, we are certain to have it.

Lindsey's Bakery is famous for baking and displaying the world's largest pumpkin pie as well. The first day it looks real pretty and smooth. But several days later there are marks all over the orangish brown filling where little kids have poked their fingers, and it becomes rather sorry-looking and disgusting.

Our parades are legendary. Bands and floats and Shriners and queens. My mama rode a float once. When she was in eleventh grade, she was Pumpkin Show Queen. Daddy has a picture of her wearing her crown. I've never seen anyone more beautiful. And that's the God's honest truth.

But what people really come to see are the pumpkins. That's what makes our festival different from any other. Right in the center of town is an area surrounded by a chain-link fence. Inside the fence is a towering treelike structure made up of regular-size pumpkins. Down from that, right in front of our circle-shaped bank, are the giants. They are eight hundred, nine hundred, sometimes even more than a thousand pounds. And there is one blue ribbon winner, the one proclaimed the largest of the large at the Pumpkin Show.

Now, as I was saying, my focus on giant pumpkins started when I was six. I don't know why. Maybe because I was too big for the kiddie rides but not brave enough for the big ones that went upside down. Things were also different for me that year. It was my first without Mama. She had died from cancer about three months before. I can remember stopping by the fenced-off display with

Daddy, and all I could think about was how Mama always used to point out the big pumpkins to me.

Daddy must have been thinking the same thing 'cause he said, "Your mama sure got a kick out of those pumpkins. Every year she would say she wanted to try her hand at growing one." He paused, and then his voice trailed off kind of sadlike. "I guess she just never got around to it."

At that very moment those big pumpkins seemed magical. I stared at their hulking forms and thought of the seeds they came from. I had helped Daddy carve a pumpkin the night before. Pumpkin seeds were flat and about the size of a fingernail. How could they grow into something so big and plump?

The people who made them grow must have some kind of special power, I decided. I felt bad because Mama never had a chance to see if she could grow one. I bet she had special powers. I bet she could have grown the biggest ever.

Then I wondered if deep inside me I might have special powers, too.

So that night I dug through the trash, looking for pumpkin seeds. I found a nice one and thought since my mama couldn't grow a giant pumpkin, I would.

Chapter 6

Aunt Arlene pulls into a parking space at the mall. She was nice enough to let me have a quiet drive up after the Arnie Bradford remark, but now she wants to talk.

"Girls your age are in the middle of changing," she says.

I immediately become self-conscious and cross my arms at my chest. I'm not really "blossoming" *that* much yet. Not like a few of the girls in my class. But what little I have I am now mightily embarrassed about. I nod to show I'm listening but stare intently at a sandwich wrapper scuttling across the parking lot in the wind.

"I think it is time for a bra," Aunt Arlene says. "And I also know clothes start to become important around this time. My brother dresses you like a boy, and I see some of the girls your age around town. They look so cute. I remember how important it was to fit in when I was your age." She pauses. "I just want to help, you know . . . since your mother can't be here."

She pats my hand, and I manage to smile at her because I don't know what else to do. I really don't care about fitting in. I have only one friend. Jacob Buckner. And he's all I really need.

I think of Jacob stopping by my house this afternoon and finding me not there. I'd much rather be playing chess with him than buying some stupid bra, and so far I really stink at chess.

Chapter 7

I suppose I should go ahead and tell the story of my first attempt at growing a pumpkin.

I had taken that nice-looking seed I had dug out of the trash, washed the orange gunk off it, and promptly put it on the nightstand beside my bed. Even at six, being a country girl, I knew you planted things in the middle of spring, when it's warm outside. So I kept that seed on my nightstand all winter long. I'd look at it each night before drifting off to sleep, and if I was lucky, I would dream giant pumpkin dreams.

In one dream I grew a pumpkin bigger than our

old farmhouse. Mama was sitting on top of that pumpkin, puffy white clouds above her head, and she was wearing her crown, and she was smiling and waving. I woke up thinking spring couldn't come quick enough. Many dreams later I finally was able to plant that little seed in the far corner of the backyard, just past where the grass was growing and weeds poked up in the surrounding field. Then I watered it good.

At the time I thought that was all there was to growing a pumpkin—planting and watering—and although I felt very pleased with myself, I told no one. I remember thinking, though, that somehow, someway Mama would know even though no one else did.

I was crazy happy when the following month, after green tendrils sprouted, some blossoms appeared. I stared hard at those pretty yellow flowers, knowing that I was the reason they came into being. I felt in control. Almost magical. And it felt tremendously good.

Before I knew it, I had five little orange balls growing on three green vines. Five pumpkins! I was expecting only one (I didn't know then that one seed could produce multiple pumpkins), so I thought I possessed special pumpkin-growing powers. In my mind I could see those five pumpkins being displayed at the Pumpkin Show come October. And I knew one of mine would be proclaimed the winner. After all, I had five chances to have the biggest pumpkin there.

Still, I told no one. I liked having a secret and wanted to keep it that way for a while. A secret just between me and my mama way up in heaven.

Not long afterward Aunt Arlene and her husband, Uncle Jerald, had me over for Sunday dinner like usual. They invited Daddy too, but he said he needed to get some yard work done. When he came to pick me up, the first thing out of his mouth was: "I almost mowed over some pumpkins. We have pumpkins growing in our backyard!"

"I know," I said. "They are from a seed I planted."

Aunt Arlene, Uncle Jerald, and Daddy looked surprised.

"I have a talent for growing pumpkins," I announced.

The grown-ups all smiled, and suddenly I was glad to share the news about my pumpkins. I felt proud of myself. I had done something important without any help at all.

Daddy tousled my hair. "Well, you'd better put some sort of marker out there or I might mow over them next time."

The next day I painted a thick wooden stick bright yellow and pushed it into the ground to keep Daddy from mowing over my pumpkins. Daddy never did mow over them, but it didn't matter. None of them got much bigger than a softball. One by one they turned mushy and rotted.

Chapter 8

Aunt Arlene sends me into the fitting room with a stretchy soft cotton bra, the smallest one to be found in the girls' section of the department store. I can remember many years ago, sitting on the floor, watching Mama fold laundry. This bra looks nothing like hers did.

"Do you know how to put it on, honey?" Aunt Arlene calls through the door. Without waiting for an answer, she explains, "Wrap it around your stomach, and close the hooks from the front. Then you can twist it around, slide your arms through the straps, and pull it up."

Gee, I think. Who knew bras could be so darn complicated? I fumble for a few moments, break into a sweat from embarrassment even though no one can see me, and finally get it on. I blow at my bangs and force myself to look in the mirror. Two grapes poking through white cotton.

"Does it fit?" Aunt Arlene asks.

"Uh-huh," I say.

"Good! We'll get a few more in that size."

Minutes later Aunt Arlene gathers up two more bras, and I start walking toward the clothes section. "Mildred," she says, "why don't we pay for these here and then look for your clothes elsewhere in the mall? We passed by a really cute boutique for girls your age. I think we will have better luck finding what we are looking for there."

What *we* are looking for? *I'm* not looking for anything special. But apparently Aunt Arlene is.

Ten minutes later we walk into the cute boutique. It's called La La Lue's. Thumping music vibrates through the store. Within seconds a girl with tight pants and hoop earrings asks if she can help us.

Aunt Arlene and the salesgirl keep on pulling clothes off the racks and asking me what I think. I always say okay because I gather it really doesn't matter one tiny bit what I think. If what I happened to think mattered, I would just be going to the discount store again with Daddy.

I do end up picking out one thing on my own, though. There's a bunch of T-shirts with sparkly words on them: *Princess*, *Spoiled*, *Sweet*. I see an orange one with the word *Pumpkin* in a fancy lettering and grab it. Not only does it catch my attention for obvious reasons, but Mama used to call me Pumpkin. She didn't care for the name Mildred either, even though that is what she named me. She named me Mildred 'cause my grandma, her mother-in-law, never cared for her when she first married Daddy, and that bothered her something awful. Mama thought if she named me after her, Grandma would like her more. Mama was very smart. It worked. Grandma was nearly as broken-hearted as Daddy and I were when Mama died.

I end up taking a whole stack of clothes into the fitting room, and Aunt Arlene and the salesgirl make me come out and model each outfit. I am mortified, but comply like the good trouper I am simply because pitching a fit would call even more attention to myself.

When I come out in jeans embroidered with flowers on the back pockets and a pink shirt with matching embroidered flowers, the salesgirl crosses her arms, shakes her head, and grins. "Your daughter is just adorable," she tells Aunt Arlene.

Aunt Arlene smiles, and with a quick apologetic look at me, she says, "Thanks." I know it would be too complicated for her to explain and also that it would make the salesgirl feel real bad if she knew I had lost my mama, so I don't mind that Aunt Arlene just told a lie.

Truth be told, Aunt Arlene did want to raise me right after Mama died. She and Uncle Jerald offered to take me in. I was upstairs at the time, supposedly asleep, but I crept downstairs a bit and heard her telling Daddy, "I only live fifteen minutes away. You'll be able to see her every day."

"No," Daddy said.

"But what if you have to make an emergency call in the middle of the night to tend to some horse or cow? What are you going to do then?"

"I'll just wake her up and take her with me. It doesn't happen often."

Aunt Arlene continued to badger Daddy until he lost his patience with her and said, "Listen, Arlene, I'm sorry you and Jerald aren't able to have any children of your own, but you're not taking mine."

I quietly eased down a few more steps and peeked through the spindles. I noticed Aunt Arlene looking real hurt. Then Daddy said in a much softer voice, "I'd be much obliged if you could watch her from time to time, but the girl is living with me in her mama's house. My office is right here, and she's not exactly a baby anymore. She's a big girl, and we'll be fine."

25

And that was the end of the story, for which I was deeply grateful. Feeling relief in the pit of my stomach, I scurried upstairs, so they wouldn't know I'd been spying. Even at six I knew that Daddy and me belonged together.

Aunt Arlene and I leave the mall with two big bags of clothes. I got the embroidered jeans with flowers on the pockets, along with four pairs of shorts, two skirts, and a bunch of coordinated tops, the pumpkin one being the only one I truly cared about.

Chapter 9

Now when those first pumpkins rotted away and died, I felt like I rotted away and died with them. Goodness, I was sad. I wasn't near as sad as I was when I lost Mama, but losing those pumpkins sure didn't help much. Growing them was the only real pleasure I had during my first year without her. I tried my best to hide those sad feelings, but Daddy noticed right away.

"Sorry about those pumpkins," he said one night at dinner, even though I hadn't told him how I was feeling.

I burst out crying. "They were going to be big. Like those ones at the Pumpkin Show."

"Well, now, growing one that big is an art form. There must be a lot more to it than putting a seed in the ground," he said.

"I took good care of them." I wiped at my tears and sniffed. "I watered them every day."

"I know, honey, but growing giant pumpkins takes hard work and special care. And probably a special kind of pumpkin seed, not one from a jack-o'-lantern."

"What kind of seed?" This news interested me.

"I'm not sure." Daddy leaned back in his chair, crossed his arms, and squinted. "We could ask Grover Fernhart. I take care of his cattle. He's been entering the big pumpkin contest for years. Usually ends up taking third or fourth place. Maybe he could give us some tips too, if you want to try again next spring."

"Yes. I want to try." I nodded my head up and down real fast.

This news made me feel much better, but I still held on to some sorrow over those pumpkins for a long time. The day before school let out for the Pumpkin Show, I couldn't help thinking about them. How I had planned to take them there and have them displayed for all to see. How Mama would be looking down from heaven, smiling. Then another person besides Daddy noticed I was sad. And that was Jacob Buckner, the boy who became my first real, true friend.

"What's wrong?" he asked. The last bell had rung, and we were walking down the hallway. Everyone else was noisy and excited, rip-roaring down the hall in excitement for having a few days off from school to ride rides and eat junk food at the Pumpkin Show. But I was all gloomy because I wouldn't have a pumpkin displayed in the middle of town for everyone to admire.

Jacob and I had never really spoken before. He was a quiet kid, not like a lot of the older boys, who always seemed to be shoving, tripping, and yelling at each other. And by the serious look on his face, he appeared to truly care. So I went ahead and told him what was wrong, even though I had to make my voice kind of loud so he could hear me.

"That's lousy," he said, like he really meant it.

We didn't immediately become best friends, but that sure laid the groundwork. I had a feeling none of the girls in my class would feel much in the way of sympathy for my rotted pumpkins.

Chapter 10

Aunt Arlene gets me, the bras, and my two bags of clothes home a little after five. She walks me in, to make sure Daddy is home. He is, but he just got back from an emergency farm call, and he smells and looks none too good. He briefly greets us and heads upstairs for a shower. Instead of leaving to go to her own house, Aunt Arlene plops herself down on our sofa.

I find this a little strange, as she usually doesn't hang around our house unless she has a reason. But I don't ask what's going on. I don't think I want to know.

When Daddy reappears fresh and clean, he

seems surprised to see her as well. He opens his mouth like he's about to say something, but Aunt Arlene interrupts him.

"Mildred," she says, sweetly, "why don't you try on the new clothes for your father? Show him what a good job we did."

Daddy can tell I'm not pleased with this idea.

"Didn't you already try those clothes on in the store?" he asks me.

"Yes," I say.

"Do you want to try them on again?"

"No."

"The girl doesn't want to try them on again," he tells Aunt Arlene.

Aunt Arlene is disappointed, I can tell. She sighs. "Well, I suppose you will see her in her new outfits sooner or later."

Daddy walks over and puts his hand on her shoulder, giving it a squeeze. "Thanks," he says. "I'm sure you handled this shopping trip a whole lot better than I could have."

After Aunt Arlene leaves, Daddy asks me to take one of his patients out for a walk, the Old English sheepdog that had been neutered in the morning.

"Puppies recover pretty quick, but since he's older, I need to keep him overnight," Daddy says.

"How old is he?" I ask.

"Nine."

"Why on earth did they wait so long to neuter him?"

"They didn't think they needed to until their neighbor decided to breed registered boxers and their female gave birth to some shaggy puppies."

"Oh!" I laugh. "Guess they learned their lesson."

"Guess so."

"Should I take Wilber and Arnold out for a walk too?"

Wilber and Arnold are our own dogs. One had been sick, and the other injured, but both had been abandoned because their owners didn't want to pay to have them treated. Daddy tried to find them homes, like he had done for other dogs, but to no avail. Wilber is a big, rangy mutt who survived a case of heartworm, and Arnold is a miniature dachshund missing his right front leg after tangling with a car.

"No," Daddy says. "The sheepdog should be taking it easy; other dogs might get him all frisky. Shirley took our two out for a romp before she left this afternoon anyway. They can wait a little longer for their turn."

The sheepdog's name is Winston. Just as I take him outside, I run into Jacob. He had ridden his bike over, and it's propped up on our sidewalk, a green helmet dangling from the handlebar. Jacob lives about a quarter of a mile away and manages to visit, unannounced, a few times a week, just like Aunt Arlene. He has a much quieter way of arriving, though. Sometimes he's around for a while before anyone even notices.

"Hey," he says, "I stopped by earlier, but you weren't here."

I wrinkle my nose. "Aunt Arlene took me shopping. Went to the north end of Columbus, so we were gone awhile." I don't mention the bras, of course.

We walk in silence for a while. We are the kind of friends that can do that. Silence doesn't bother us. We aren't jabberboxes, and perhaps that is why we get along so well. Gloria Mathis, the girl who plasters her notebooks with pictures of her actor crush, is a jabberbox, and not to be mean, but honestly, even though lots of girls hang on her every word, I can only stand a few minutes in her presence.

Considering Winston's age and the fact he is recovering from surgery, he *is* frisky. He keeps pulling on the leash, and my poor arm feels as though it is being pulled out of the socket. Besides being frisky, Winston is one big dog.

"Want me to take him for a bit?" Jacob asks.

"Sure." I hand the leash over. Jacob handles Winston like he is no big deal. Jacob is only a year older than I am, but he is taller than Daddy, and Daddy is not a short man. We wind our way to the backyard.

I stop by the sacred place. I already prepared the brown soil in late March by turning it. It contains compost, rotted cow manure, and even some molasses to attract earthworms. Right now it kind of looks as if one of our dogs had a good time digging a huge circle, about thirty feet in diameter, in our otherwise green lawn.

While I admire my dirt, Jacob walks Winston around a little more, making sure he does his business. He even goes ahead and cleans it up without my saying a word. Jacob has always been the helpful sort. But there is one thing he has never helped me with, and that is growing my pumpkin. I have allowed him to watch the past three years—the years I turned eight, nine, and ten—but he knows better than to even offer to water any vine that sprouts from that patch of ground. It's something I have to be solely responsible for, and he understands that despite the fact I've never discussed this with him. He just knows.

Jacob leads Winston over my way and stands

beside me. Winston wants to explore and sniff some more, but Jacob holds him steady, and the dog finally gives up and sits.

He and I both stare at the patch of dirt.

"Today's April seventeenth," he says. "Won't be long until you get to plant it here."

"Yep," I say.

"Maybe this will finally be the year," he says.

"Maybe."

I know, though, not to get my hopes up. Four growing seasons—if you include the one where I used a jack-o'-lantern seed—and I still haven't grown a pumpkin I thought worth displaying at the Pumpkin Show.

I set up the chessboard on the kitchen table. I love how the game pieces are different and represent real figures—kings, queens, bishops, knights. My favorite is the knight because it looks like a horse's head. But even though I'm intrigued by the pieces, I'm having a hard time understanding how to play.

Jacob has been trying to teach me for the past four months, and I still have to interrupt the game to ask a ton of questions.

Daddy asks Jacob if he wants to stay for dinner.

"Depends on what you're having." Jacob grins. Daddy isn't exactly the world's greatest cook, but he tries.

"Bacon, lettuce, and tomato sandwiches with chips on the side," Daddy says.

"That sounds safe," Jacob says. "I'll stay."

Daddy starts frying the bacon, and with the game board all set up, Jacob and I start playing chess.

Ten minutes later the bacon's done and Daddy's slicing the tomatoes. And I start to make a move that causes Jacob to shake his head. "Can't do that," he says quietly, without even a hint of exasperation in his voice.

I sigh, returning the piece. Jacob never gets upset with me. He has so much patience. Well, either that or he is just plain stubborn. You'd think by now he would have given up on my ever learning the game. But then I guess I can be pretty stubborn myself. I move another piece.

"Check," Jacob says.

By the time Daddy sets down our plates with triangle-sliced BLTs, the game is over. Jacob has said the dreaded "checkmate."

I take a bite of my sandwich. "Think I'll ever be able to beat you?" I ask.

"Yes," Jacob says. "But I wouldn't count on it happening anytime soon."

Chapter 11

On Monday I wear my new T-shirt with the sparkly word *Pumpkin* and an above-the-knee yellow skirt that Aunt Arlene picked out to go with it. I feel a little funny because I'm wearing a bra too. It doesn't feel natural, but I suppose I'll get used to it.

At breakfast Daddy says, "You look nice, but that skirt seems like it could be just a smidgen longer."

The skirt really isn't *that* short, but it's been years since Daddy has seen me in anything that resembles a dress. It must look a little strange.

I shrug. "Aunt Arlene and the saleslady say it's what all the girls are wearing."

"Are they?"

"I don't know. I've never really paid attention to what other girls wear. You want me to go upstairs and put on one of my old pairs of jeans?"

Daddy blows on his hot coffee and takes a sip. "No. I guess I'll just trust Aunt Arlene's judgment."

I would have actually been happy to change the skirt, but I'm guessing Daddy's response really isn't about trusting Aunt Arlene's judgment.

"What?" I grin. "Are you afraid Aunt Arlene will stop by the second I get home from school? Just to make sure I'm putting my new clothes to good use?"

Daddy grins back at me. "Heaven knows it wouldn't be worth the trouble it would cause me and you if she caught you coming home from school in your old jeans."

Sometimes Daddy and me joke about Aunt Arlene, but we're being more affectionate than mean. Yes, Aunt Arlene gets on our nerves royally, but she's one of the few relatives we've got. She's Daddy's only sibling, and I have no relatives on Mama's side. Well, at least that I know of. Mama was placed in foster care when she was eight because her mother was neglecting her.

Mama started explaining the whole thing to me when I was a baby and not really able to understand. So by the time I was old enough to notice I didn't have a second pair of grandparents, I already knew the reason why. It didn't come as a big shock because I knew the circumstances from before I could even remember.

Mama always said her past didn't bother her and she didn't mind not growing up with a real family. She told me all that mattered was that she had me and Daddy, and that more than made up for everything.

But of course now we don't have her. And it really, truly stinks.

When I get to school, Gloria Mathis and some of the other girls take a sudden interest in me. They all gather around my desk.

"Whoa! Who gave you a makeover?" Gloria asks. "You look good!"

I remember the second year I tried growing a giant pumpkin, I made an effort to get the girls in my class interested in me. I was confident things would go well this time, and since Daddy and Aunt Arlene already knew about my pumpkin growing and it wasn't a secret like my first attempt, I thought I would share the news of my wonderful project with them.

"I'm growing a pumpkin," I told them at recess. "A giant one. For the Pumpkin Show."

But Gloria had painted her fingernails purple the night before, and everyone seemed much more interested in her purple fingernails than in my pumpkin.

I didn't have much time to be hurt, though.

Jacob was nearby; his arm was in a cast, and he was watching some of the other boys shooting hoops. He had overheard me and seemed interested right away.

"I remember how sad you looked last October," he said. "I wondered if you would try again."

After talking pumpkins for a while, I pointed at his cast. "What happened to your arm?"

"I fell off my bike," he said. He raised his good arm in the air. "Luckily, I write with this hand, though."

After that, the two of us started talking on a regular basis during recess. I thought maybe once Jacob got his cast off he would go back to playing with the boys in his class, but that never happened. He stuck with me.

Anyway, now the very girls who couldn't care less about me *growing* a pumpkin were raving about my pumpkin shirt.

"Did you get it from La La Lue's?" Alicia Weber asked. "I loooove that shop! It's soooo expensive, though. My mom doesn't let me shop there very often."

I nod and admit I got the T-shirt from La La Lue's. I'm aware that I should be pleased with their attention. Aunt Arlene would be pleased, I know. I should be bragging about wearing a bra, too. That seems to be the thing to do in fifth grade. But all I can think about is how close it is to pumpkin-growing season, so I busy myself with putting the books I used for homework back in my desk.

Chapter 12

When I get home from school on Tuesday, I go through the office door. Sometimes I catch Daddy between animal exams hanging around the front desk, but today there's only Shirley. "Tell Dad I'm home," I say. She nods, and I go outside again and through our "regular" front door.

Wilber and Arnold are happy to see me, Wilber leaning against my thigh and Arnold racing around my legs with his three feet. Missing one leg doesn't slow him down much. I grab their leashes, hung from pegs on the wall in the entryway, and give them a quick walk. Afterward I head up to my room.

Even though I have to wait awhile to dig a hole in the soil I have prepared out back, this day is a very important one in my quest to grow a giant pumpkin.

I take a seed packet, containing Dill's Atlantic Giant seeds, from my desktop. I found out about Dill's Atlantic Giant after my disastrous first attempt to grow a pumpkin. It was a few weeks after the Pumpkin Show, and Daddy made good on his promise to talk to Grover Fernhart, the cattle farmer who grew giant pumpkins. One of his cows had a problem, so off we went.

We drove down his long driveway, past a fenced-in field of Herefords with their red bodies and white faces. Daddy parked in front of Grover's barn. "You want to come along and help?" he asked.

"What are you doing?" Sometimes I enjoyed the work Daddy did. Especially since he had started letting me help a bit. The week before I had acted as an assistant when he gelded a quarter horse. He would point at and describe whatever he needed, and I would hand it over to him. A pretty big deal for a seven-year-old.

"I'm removing cancer eye," he said.

"Will the cow be okay?" I asked.

"The cow will be okay, but once it heals Grover will have to send her to market. Can't keep a cow for breeding once it has cancer eye. It's hereditary, so it could be passed along to offspring."

"Don't think I want to watch you then." I shook my head. "It would be too sad to see her, knowing she's headed to be butchered."

"Okay. We'll find something else for you to do while I'm busy. After I'm done, you can ask Grover for some tips on growing those big pumpkins."

By then Grover Fernhart was heading our way. We got out of the truck, and Daddy took some equipment boxes out of the back.

"It's a shame," Grover said, adjusting his green farmer's cap lower on his forehead. "She was a nice one. But what can you do?"

While Daddy took care of the doomed cow, I

busied myself with some kittens in the nearby hay barn. Some of them were wild, but a few came crawling into my lap. It was a nice way to wait.

Half an hour later Daddy was done. Grover Fernhart and I stood beside the truck as Daddy put his equipment boxes back in.

"Mildred here is thinking about trying her hand at growing one of those giant pumpkins," Daddy said.

Grover looked at me and smirked, which I did not appreciate. Then he looked at Daddy and started talking like I wasn't even there. "I think she's too young," he said. "Growing those big ones is labor-intensive. Don't think she'll have the time or patience for it. It's almost like taking care of a newborn baby; they require a heck of a lot of tender loving care. I swear if I started telling her how to go about it now, I wouldn't be done till next Sunday."

I stared up at Daddy as earnestly as I could. "I don't care how much work it takes. I want to grow one."

"Can't you at least let us know what kind of seed you need?" Daddy asked.

"Howard Dill's Atlantic Giant." Grover stuffed his hands in the front pockets of his tan overalls. "No one grows the truly big ones without using Howard Dill's Atlantic Giant."

Chapter 13

I take ten seeds out of the packet, and using a fingernail file, I saw the rounded edges of each one until the interior is slightly exposed. This will help moisture get in for germination.

I took great care in selecting and buying these seeds. Atlantic Giants have pedigrees, just like purebred dogs. There are records of the mothers and fathers and the average weight of the pumpkins they produce. Sometimes you can even trace back six or seven generations. My seeds came from a 1361 Keplar (female parent) and a 910 Stevens (male pollinator).

The number indicates the weight of the pumpkin, and the name is the last name of the person who grew it.

I plant the seeds, pointed side down, in peat pots filled with good-quality potting soil; add water; then place the pots on a small table near my bedroom window. Under the pots is a germination mat, which will provide heat for the seeds until they sprout from the soil. Eventually I will transplant the best-looking one to the patch outside.

I say a little prayer of thanks to Howard Dill and his generosity. The man spent thirty years developing giant pumpkins and was able to break a seventy-five-year-old world record for biggest pumpkin in 1979. He continued as world champion for three more years. Instead of keeping his seeds and the glory that went with them to himself, he decided to share them with anyone he could. He got the seeds patented and started selling them to the public. All big pumpkins owe their existence to him. So all those pumpkins my mama enjoyed looking at can be traced back to Howard Dill.

And now I've got his seeds in ten pots beside my bedroom window. Even though Mama's not here anymore, it kind of makes me feel close to her.

The rest of the week at school, most of the girls are nicer than usual to me. I think it is on account of my new wardrobe. But it's hard for me to act interested back at them. For one thing, I figure I gave them a chance way back when, and they really didn't want to get to know me. Truth be told, I think they still don't want to know the real me. Besides, all I can think about are my seeds. First thing I do when I get home every day is check on them.

On Saturday morning I'm ecstatic. I've got seedlings! Six of them have pushed through the soil and are visible.

I get dressed, grab a quick breakfast of cereal, and go into Daddy's office. He is there, going over the day's schedule with Shirley. Their heads are bent close together, and I notice Shirley has a new haircut. It makes her look even prettier than usual. Aunt

Arlene keeps on bugging Daddy to ask her out, but Daddy as usual just ignores the advice.

"Anything I can do?" I ask.

"The cages need to be cleaned and disinfected," Daddy says without looking up.

"Okay!" I reply a little too happily.

They both pop their heads up to give me a questioning look.

"I've already got *six* good prospects," I explain.

They know what I'm talking about.

"Maybe this will be the year," Shirley says.

"Maybe," I reply.

By Sunday morning three more seeds have sprouted. That makes nine—my best germination rate ever. Looks as if only one might be a dud.

Late afternoon Daddy and I go to Aunt Arlene's for dinner. She is serving homemade fried chicken, real mashed potatoes, and canned green beans that came from her little garden out back. Aunt Arlene is an excellent cook, and I have to say I always manage to enjoy dinner at her house, but this one gets off to a rocky start when Daddy shares the news of my successful seedlings.

He is happy things are going well for me so far. Probably because he has always shared my disappointment when things have gone wrong. He has a big smile on his face, one that almost matches mine.

Aunt Arlene is not smiling, though. She was about to stuff some green beans in her mouth but instead lets her fork fall to her plate. "I can't believe you're letting her do it again. How could you? She always ends up heartbroken, you know that. The girl needs other interests."

I don't appreciate her scolding Daddy like that, and I'm about to tell her so, but she suddenly turns her attention to me. "Mildred, honey, you've got to stop this nonsense. You spend way too much of your time fretting over those pumpkins. Your whole summer ends up being consumed with it when you should be having fun."

"But it *is* fun!" I say.

"It's an obsession. I've told you that before. It's not healthy."

"Daddy!" I wanted to defend him a moment ago; now I'm pleading for his help.

"Leave the girl alone. It's a hobby she loves. There's nothing wrong with that," Daddy says.

"Yeah, you grow things too!" I scoop up some green beans to show her. I am tempted to fling them her way, but don't have the courage to. "You spend lots of time in your garden, and you also put in a lot of work canning things."

"It's different. I have outside interests. I have volunteer work. I belong to several ladies' groups." She sighs. "It's not my intention to be mean. I just want what's best for you."

I open my mouth to say something else, but Uncle Jerald, who's normally quiet, pipes up. "Can we please spend the rest of dinner in peace? The food's getting cold while you are all busy arguing."

The arguing does stop, but the rest of dinner

happens to be uncomfortably quiet. Just the clink of silverware hitting plates.

Later, when Daddy and I are getting ready to leave, Aunt Arlene comes over and gives me a hug and a kiss on the cheek, like always. I can't help but be stiff as a board. She looks hurt, and I feel bad, but not bad enough to say I'm sorry.

Chapter 14

Jacob comes over after school on Thursday. Even though he's stopped by and seen them before, I proudly show him again the sprouts from nine of my pots. The remaining one never did poke through the soil, and by now I've given up on it. But nine sprouts happens to be pretty darn good.

For the past two years I've ended up with maybe seven or so of them germinating successfully. This is the first year I've used an extra source of heat from the germination mat, and I think the heat it produced has helped, since seeds like soil temps of about eighty degrees. But now that there are tiny leaves showing, they need sunlight and cooler soil, so I've removed the heat source.

Jacob admires each sprout. "Maybe we should place bets on which one you'll end up planting outside."

I laugh. "You know I'd plant them all if I could. But Daddy says we wouldn't have any backyard left then. I guess it's for the best, though. I like being devoted to one plant, giving it my all. I couldn't properly take care of nine of them."

Suddenly Wilber comes bounding into the room and tries to shove his way between Jacob and me so he can be the center of attention. He knocks Jacob off-balance. All I can do is watch in horror as my friend crashes into and overturns the small table holding all my precious seedlings.

Jacob scrambles to his feet, looking grief-stricken. "Oh, gawd, Mildred."

I start screaming my head off at Wilber, but the poor dog seems confused by all the chaos and ends up trampling the dirt and green sprouts littering the floor. "Wilber, no!" I drop to the ground, desperately trying to scoop up and protect my baby plants, but Wilber, knowing he is in some sort of trouble, wants forgiveness, so he keeps on licking my face and getting in the way.

Jacob comes to the rescue, grabbing Wilber by his collar and hustling him out to the hallway. After closing the door on him, Jacob sprints over to where I am and begins to help me put dirt and sprouts back into the peat pots.

By the time we're finished, and the pots line the table again, it's evident most won't make it: tiny new leaves torn and ripped, stems broken, just pitiful-looking.

"I'm so sorry, Mildred." Jacob hangs his head, and I can tell he is on the verge of crying.

I want to cry too, but I don't want Jacob feeling any worse than he already does. "It's not your fault. It's not even Wilber's; he was just being friendly," I say. And even though there is anger boiling in me,

I know the words are true. It was just an awful, terrible accident.

"Do you think a few of them will be all right?" Jacob asks hopefully.

"I think three of them look okay. It's not a total loss. I'll still be able to plant one out back." But as I say that, I can't help wondering if perhaps the *one* destined for greatness has been destroyed.

Jacob sticks around for a while, and we play a few games of chess. He lets me win one game, in an attempt to make me feel better, but I call him on it.

"This game doesn't count. You let me win on purpose," I say.

He doesn't argue with me. Just looks at me with a real sad expression, and it makes me wish I hadn't said anything, that I just would have accepted the win with a smile on my face.

After he leaves, I pitch the six ruined plants in the trash. Then I flop onto my bed and have a good, long, hard cry while holding my pillow.

Even though I'm sick to my stomach over what happened, I try to be extra nice to Wilber for the rest of the evening. I feel bad about screaming at him 'cause I know he meant no harm. Before heading up to bed, I take the time to rub his belly, something he dearly loves. Arnold gets jealous, hobbles over, and tries to climb in my lap. So with my free hand, I scratch him behind his ear. "Why couldn't it have been you that came bounding into the room, little guy?" I ask. "No way could you have knocked Jacob down."

I go and find Daddy in the kitchen. He is poring over some veterinarian journal while he's munching on a cookie.

"Good night," I say.

"Good night, sweetie." He stands up and hugs me, kissing the top of my head. "Sorry about those sprouts you lost."

I shrug.

Once in bed, I stare at the three plants I have left, their outlines silhouetted by moonlight in the darkened room. One of them is drooping pretty badly. I thought I would have nine to choose from, but now it looks as though there will only be two.

And I can't help thinking Aunt Arlene was right about one thing: My past pumpkin-growing efforts have always left me with a broken heart. And maybe this time I will end up with a broken heart too. Still, it's something I feel I have to do. I have to try, and it just wouldn't feel right if I up and quit.

Chapter 15

On Saturday Daddy asks if I want to go with him to help pull a calf.

"Sure," I say. Sometimes mama cows have a hard time delivering their babies, and they have to be pulled out. I like seeing freshly born calves. I like seeing them take their first wobbly steps. It's as if I'm witnessing a little miracle. Sometimes the calf is born dead, though. That's dreadful sad to see. But most of the time things turn out just fine, so it's worth the risk.

We are well on our way, rattling down a country

road, when I ask what farm we are going to.

"Grover Fernhart's," Daddy says.

"Oh, Daddy, I don't want to see *him*. Why didn't you tell me?"

"What's wrong with Grover?"

"He always asks me about my pumpkin growing. Then he gets all smug and starts bragging about how big his last one was."

"But he was the one who told you about Dill's Atlantic Giant. You have to give him that."

"I guess." I stare out the window, purple wild-flowers blurring as we speed along.

The second year I tried growing a big pumpkin, I used the right seed, thanks to Grover. But I thought he was just trying to frighten me off with his declaration of all the hard work and time involved. I thought he was scared I'd grow a bigger pumpkin than he could. Here I was a little just-turned-eight-year-old, and I was sure he didn't want me to try because I'd be competition. So all I did was put one seed in the ground and gave it a good dose of water.

Not long after, I had seen my aunt Arlene use something called Miracle-Gro in her garden. She explained it helped fertilize the plants so they would be strong and healthy.

Well, I got me some Miracle-Gro too. I thought it was my secret weapon. And I did end up growing nice pumpkins. Four altogether, weighing 111 pounds, 123 pounds, 144 pounds, and 170 pounds. I knew they weren't near large enough to enter the contest, though, so Daddy and I ended up carving them, and they lined our front porch for Halloween. Got lots of compliments on them, and Daddy always proudly told people how I had grown those pumpkins. But I knew compared with the ones I had seen at the Pumpkin Show, they were pipsqueaks, and I felt like a failure. Couldn't even properly enjoy trick or treat that year. Jacob went with me, both of us dressed as hoboes, and I couldn't help thinking that every smiling jack-o'-lantern I encountered was putting me down.

And now I have to go see Grover Fernhart, knowing he will be just as smug as those jack-o'-lanterns. Always acting like I don't stand a chance of growing a decent giant pumpkin just because I'm not a grown-up.

Chapter 16

The sun is shining on Grover's farm. He has a huge yellow farmhouse, a big red barn, and miles of white fence. I can't deny it's a pretty place. Daddy's humming and grinning beside me as we fly down the gravel drive, kicking up dust, and I find myself happy to be tagging along with him despite my feelings toward Grover.

When Grover approaches us, he seems so concerned with his cow that he doesn't much notice me, for which I'm grateful. He leads us behind the barn. The mama cow is already restrained in a cattle chute, so Daddy can attend to her. One little hoof is sticking out under her tail. A problem, because I know calves should come out with *both* front hooves and their noses first.

Some farmers are quite good at pulling calves, but Daddy told me on the way over that Grover is a real nervous Nellie at the first sign of trouble. Grover is showing his nervousness now, pacing back and forth.

Daddy slips on some long plastic gloves. Then he pats the cow's hip and lifts her tail. He slides his arm inside her, feeling around for the position of the calf.

"Which hoof is sticking out, front or back?" Grover asks anxiously.

I start to worry too. I hold my breath.

"Front," Daddy says. "And the calf is alive. The knee is bent on its other front leg. Just need to straighten the leg out and pull the hoof up next to the other one, so I think we're in good shape."

Grover and I let out sighs of relief.

Daddy pulls out the other front hoof. He loops a chain with handles around each hoof. Daddy takes one handle and asks me to pull the other, so Grover can catch the calf.

"Really?" I ask, surprised.

"The calf is in a good position. Should come out easy now. And listen, how many calf pullings have you watched? You'll do fine."

We both lean backward, me straining a bit more than Daddy. The calf's nose appears, and once the shoulder can be seen, the rest slips out. Grover quickly cradles the body and eases the wet baby to the ground.

"A heifer," Grover says.

I'm glad she's a girl. Maybe she can lead a long life of having babies.

Grover rubs the calf, and Daddy puts his fingers in the calf's mouth and nose to clear out fluid. Then he tickles the calf's nose with a piece of straw to get her breathing.

The mama is released, and we stand back and

watch as she licks her baby with her rough tongue.

Grover, whom I have seldom seen smile, has a huge grin on his face. For a moment I almost feel a bond with him. We have been through a calf birthing together, both of us worried and now happy.

But Grover has to ruin it. He turns his attention away from his new calf. "Growing another one this year?" he asks.

"Yes, Mr. Fernhart." I call him Mr. Fernhart to his face, out of politeness. But to me, he has always been just Grover. A fellow grower and competitor. Someone on the same playing field as I am.

"Hope you got your seed sprouted already."

"Uh-huh." Did he think I was stupid?

"Want to see mine?"

I want to say no but can't resist. "Sure."

I guess Grover must have figured I was hopeless, having failed to produce anything for the Pumpkin Show since he first talked to me over three years ago. He doesn't seem to be very concerned about my stealing any of his secrets.

"I've been at this twenty years now," Grover tells us, nodding. "Never have taken first place. But this will be *my* year. I can feel it in my bones."

Daddy and I follow him to the back of the yellow farmhouse and over to the first of three nice-looking greenhouses.

"I'm planting mine outside tomorrow," I say. "Did you just get yours in the ground?"

"Planted mine just as soon as they sprouted," Grover says. "Over a week ago."

"Weren't you afraid of frost?" I ask, incredulous that Grover could be so dumb as to plant his so young and tender outside, even if he did have green-houses set up.

Grover seems sincerely surprised that I had any knowledge at all about planting. He squints at me in silence for a moment. Finally says, kind of huffylike, "No, I'm not afraid of frost. I've buried heating cables. The ground doesn't get cold that way."

"Oh," was all I could manage to say, and I really did feel stupid. I have heard about heating cables, but they seem too complicated and expensive for me to use. I peek into each greenhouse, take in his glorious-looking sprouts, and wonder how on earth I can compete against Grover Fernhart.

By Grover's expression, I can tell he is thinking the same thing. But instead of feeling discouraged, it ends up making me even more determined.

Chapter 17

Sunday, May 2. My eleventh birthday. As soon as I wake up, I study the two leafy plants on my table. It's an easy choice. The one near my bed is bigger and more hardy-looking. I decide to transplant that one to my patch in the backyard.

I carefully carry the pot to the garage, and with my free hand I pick up my gardening box and head outside. Ten days ago I covered my prepared soil with a square of black plastic to soak up the sun's warmth and dry the ground underneath. Not as fancy as Grover Fernhart's underground heating cables, but it did the job just fine. The black plastic covers the top of a small hill that's about ten feet wide and a foot high in the middle. I created the mound to aid with drainage.

I remove the black plastic covering and dig into the center of the mound. I stick my plant in the newly created hole, gently pushing dirt around it. Standing back, I admire what I have just done. I know the really hard work is yet to come, but I let some satisfaction sink in. It looks real good.

I go back to the garage and get three half-inch, ten-foot-long PVC pipes, which I haul back to my patch. I stick the end of one pipe six inches into the ground. Then I bend the pipe over and stick the other end into the ground as well. This forms an arch over my plant area. I do the same with the other two pipes, placing them about thirty inches apart. Now I have a frame that I can cover with Reemay, a cloth that lets sun, moisture, and heat in but keeps bugs out. At night I will add a plastic sheet for additional warmth. This temporary hoop house will protect my plant from the wind and weather for a while longer since it's still fairly delicate and vulnerable at this stage.

Jacob knows it's planting day, so he shows up in the afternoon to see what I've done. He nods in approval. And I feel full of anticipation for the growing season ahead.

We end up playing a few games of chess. Once it actually took him longer than fifteen minutes to beat me. I'm improving, I think.

Jacob stays for dinner, and afterward I have my birthday party. Aunt Arlene has brought a white cake with pink roses she baked and decorated herself. It is on one end of the kitchen table, and my gifts are on the other. Besides Jacob, Aunt Arlene, and Daddy, Uncle Jerald is here too. They sing "Happy Birthday" and have me blow out my candles. I make my wish. One that has to do with my pumpkin plant, of course.

The cake is scrumptious—moist strawberry cake inside—and Wilber and Arnold make pests of themselves, watching every forkful and hoping for crumbs to fall. When it is time to open gifts, I go for Daddy's first. Two large boxes tied together with ribbon. One contains a new soaker hose for watering, and the other has three different types of fertilizer for the different stages of pumpkin growth. I smile. "Thanks. Just what I wanted."

"I know." Daddy laughs. "You gave me a list."

Growing pumpkins can be expensive, and the allowance I get for doing chores and helping Daddy goes only so far. The seed alone took up a nice chunk of my money.

"Fertilizer! You asked for fertilizer?" Aunt Arlene rolls her eyes but is kind enough to refrain from further comment, so as not to ruin my party.

I open Jacob's next. A gift certificate to play putt-putt golf.

"I'll beat you," he says.

"Yeah, right." I punch his arm. "You might have an advantage with chess, but I'm no pushover when it comes to putt-putt."

The only gift left is from Aunt Arlene and Uncle Jerald. It is a small, square gift, and when I open it, I discover tiny diamond earrings.

"They're real," Aunt Arlene says.

"But I don't have pierced ears!"

"Not yet. I'm taking you to get them pierced on Saturday."

Aunt Arlene seems totally pleased with herself. Lots of girls in my class have their ears pierced, but I've never really thought about it. I'm about to protest that I don't want my ears pierced, but then I remember seeing some pumpkin earrings last year at a jewelry stand during the Pumpkin Show. Maybe, I think, I could get a pair. A pair to celebrate my having the biggest pumpkin at the Pumpkin Show this year.

"They're beautiful," I say. "Thanks." I look over at Jacob. He doesn't seem too impressed by the earrings. And the truth is, I'm not either. I wrinkle my nose at him, and he tries not to laugh.

Chapter 18

A sick, crackling noise zips through my head. I let out a yelp, and it's all I can do to keep from jumping out of the tall chair I'm sitting in.

"I'm not getting the other one done!" I tell Aunt Arlene.

Instead of offering sympathy, she laughs. "Your mother said the same exact thing when I took her to get her ears pierced."

I forget about my stinging left ear for a moment. "You took Mama to get her ears pierced?"

"Yes. She mentioned she wanted them pierced

before her wedding day, so I took her."

I want to ask why she waited so long and why Aunt Arlene took her, but the ear-piercing lady is looking pretty impatient. "So," she says, tapping her foot, "should I do the other ear or not?"

I knew Mama must have gone ahead and gotten her other ear done because I remember her always wearing a pair of tiny birthstone earrings Daddy got her. She wasn't one for dangly, flashy stuff, like what the ear-piercing lady is wearing now. She's shaking her head as she's waiting for my answer, and her earrings are slapping at her neck.

"Go ahead," I say, and I feel my body stiffen in anticipation of the pain about to come. Since Mama was brave enough to go through with it, I will too. Anyway, I'd feel kind of lopsided having only one done.

After we leave the mall, Aunt Arlene decides to take me to lunch at some fancy restaurant.

I put the heavy cloth napkin on my lap and study

the menu. Really, I would have been just as happy to go to McDonald's. Aunt Arlene is always trying to impress me, for some unknown reason. It never works. I study the menu, and when the waiter comes, I tell him I want the chicken salad croissant sandwich and raspberry lemonade.

Aunt Arlene grins like I have passed some sort of test and orders the same.

While we're waiting for our food, I go ahead and ask Aunt Arlene why Mama waited so long to have her ears pierced.

"I think her being raised in foster care had something to do with it. Just wasn't a priority, and she didn't want to have to ask anyone to take her, I guess. When she got engaged, she was going to go all by herself, but I offered to take her and come along for support."

"You went to high school with Daddy and Mama, right?" I ask.

"Yes. Two years ahead of them."

"And they were high school sweethearts," I say.

"Started dating each other their sophomore year." Aunt Arlene nods.

I pause for a moment, scrunching up my face and trying to gain the courage to ask something important. Finally I say, "I know what Mama was like as my mama. But what was she like before that?"

"Hasn't your daddy talked to you about that?"

"No."

Aunt Arlene frowns, and I expect her to say something snide about Daddy. But all at once her expression goes soft. "Must be too hard for him to talk about that yet. Well, let me see here. . . . Your mama was pretty and smart and as sweet as they come. She was popular. A star volleyball player. She could jump and spike the ball like no one else. And she was funny. She had a knack for telling awful jokes, and somehow people would always laugh instead of groan. You'd think being in foster care would have made people look down on her, but she was special, and there was no denying that. Everyone loved her."

"Everyone except Grandma. She didn't like her back then."

"How did you know that?" Aunt Arlene seems surprised.

"I used to hear Mama and Daddy talking about it a lot. And how happy it made them when her feelings finally changed," I say.

Aunt Arlene gives me a funny look. "Little ears hear big things, it seems."

"So how come Grandma didn't like her?" I ask.

"Well, your grandma thought being in foster care meant she wasn't being raised right. But your mother had three foster families since she was eight, and according to her, they were all fine folks who treated her decent."

I knew that already. Daddy told me her first foster family moved to California when she turned twelve, and they weren't allowed to take her with them. Daddy still gets letters from them every once in a while. An older woman took care of her next— they became very close—but then she died of a heart attack when Mama was almost seventeen. So Mr. and Mrs. Petroskie took over. Daddy and I sometimes see the two of them around town. They always seem happy to see me and will stop to chat a bit, but they didn't really have Mama that long. Not long enough to seem like family.

"So you're saying Grandma felt bad toward Mama 'cause she was a foster kid? That's not fair." I lean forward and put my elbows on the table, then suddenly wonder if I'm going to get yelled at for doing so. But Aunt Arlene leans closer to me and puts her elbows on the table, too.

"Your grandma also thought your mother was way too pretty to be a good wife. But after she married your father, she started helping him with his veterinary practice. And when your grandma saw her wearing overalls covered with blood and manure one day, she began to see the light." Aunt Arlene starts smiling real big.

"And then I was born," I say, and I'm smiling real big right along with Aunt Arlene.

"Yes, and that was the icing on the cake. From then on my mother and yours got along famously." Aunt Arlene reaches across the table and gives my hand a squeeze.

Even though I'm hungry, I'm sorry to see the waiter at our table, placing our plates of food down, because our conversation is interrupted.

When he leaves, Aunt Arlene takes a bite out of her sandwich and asks how my ears are feeling.

"Sore," I say.

After we are done eating, Aunt Arlene asks if I want to go anywhere else since we are in Columbus.

"No, I have to go home to check on my pumpkin plant," I tell her.

I hear a very long sigh coming from Aunt Arlene, which I do my best to ignore.

Chapter 19

It's the third week of June, a beautiful evening, close to dusk. While crickets chirp in the background, I carefully tie paper bags around two of my female buds. I can tell they are females because of the small yellow bulge between the bud and stem. The yellow bulge is a baby pumpkin, and it will grow only if pollination is successful. The buds will be opening soon into bright, pretty flowers, and the bags covering them will keep bees from depositing pollen from other plants. I will be hand pollinating them myself. I place bags over the males I will be using too.

I stand up and take a good look at my pumpkin plant. Hundreds of healthy green leaves now. Stretching vines I have buried with dirt. It has long outgrown the little hoop house I placed over it after planting. And also the conservation fence that replaced it for wind protection.

When school let out a few weeks back, I felt like kicking up my heels. More time to tend to my pumpkin plant! Once I got it in the ground, I hated being away for a good portion of the day. Now I'm able to putter around my plant to my heart's content. It's heaven.

As soon as I go back inside the house, I hear the phone ringing and then Daddy's voice saying, "Just a minute . . ."

I enter the kitchen, and Daddy tells me I have a phone call.

It's Jacob, but I knew that already. He's the only one who ever calls me.

"Hey," I say.

"Hey," he replies. "One of my dad's coworkers

gave him four tickets to Cedar Point. Since that means we have one extra, want to go?"

"When?" I do love roller coasters, so I'm tempted.

"Tomorrow."

"When are you leaving?"

"Like five in the morning, so we can make the four-hour trip to get there when it opens."

"Can't. I have some females ready to open up and pollinate; there's only a four- to six-hour window that it can be done. I need to stay home."

Jacob doesn't give me a hard time, even though I can tell he is disappointed.

I wonder what Aunt Arlene would think. My choosing my pumpkin plant over an amusement park. Don't think I really want to know.

I hang up the phone and head for bed. I'll be up at the crack of dawn, and tomorrow's a big day. But I can hardly wait; pollinating is just as exciting to me as screaming my head off on some roller coaster.

Chapter 20

Fortunately, it's a nice, warm, but not too hot morning. Just right for the job ahead. Anything over ninety degrees, and I would have to cool the females with frozen water-filled bottles, which would be a pain. I have already taken off the paper bags, and the two female blossoms are wide open and ready.

I find a strong-looking male blossom and cut it from the stem. I pull off the petals until all that's left is the stamen. Using the stamen like a paintbrush, I rub pollen on the inside stigma of the female flower. I repeat the process, using a couple of stamens on each stigma. And I know, during the next two weeks I will be doing this over and over as more females get ready. But I don't mind. What I am doing is giving these baby pumpkins a chance to grow. Perhaps into a real, true giant.

By the time I head inside, Daddy is already in his office, getting things ready for the day.

"What can I do to help?" I ask.

"You know the beagle pup with the broken leg?"

I nod.

"Her owners called this morning. They won't be picking her up today. They decided they didn't want to pay the bill. I offered to set up an installment plan and a discount, but they didn't seem interested in working with me. They asked if I could find her a new home."

"Are we keeping her?" I ask.

"I hope not. She's young—about nine weeks old—and still needs to be housebroken and trained. She'd take up a lot of time. I thought maybe you could bring her out to the waiting room. Show her to everyone that comes in. Maybe someone will want her . . . or they'll know someone who will."

I go get the beagle pup out of her cage, careful of the back right leg that's bandaged. She snuggles into my chest, and I stroke her head. She's so sweet! Part of me wishes we could keep her, but I think of Daddy's warning of the time she'd take up. Puppies have to be watched constantly because they chew things like furniture and shoes, and they have to be taken out all the time so they can learn not to do their business inside the house. With my pumpkins and helping out Daddy this summer, I wouldn't have enough time to devote to her.

I show the pup to everyone who walks in during the next few hours. Everyone makes a fuss over her and pets her, but no takers. Finally Mrs. Goldmeyer, an English teacher from the high school, comes in. She's struggling, carrying a very sick-looking old dog in her arms, a Lab mix that Daddy has been treating for leukemia.

Shirley comes out from behind the counter and

takes the dog from her arms. "I'll take him on back," she says.

Mrs. Goldmeyer follows Shirley back to an exam room. "It's time," she says, and I hear her begin to sob.

Fifteen minutes later Daddy walks Mrs. Goldmeyer out, his arm about her shoulder. Mrs. Goldmeyer has a tissue in her hand, but her dog is nowhere in sight. I know what has happened. It's the part of Daddy's practice that makes me sad. Him too.

I don't have the heart to talk to her about the beagle. Daddy catches my eye and shakes his head sternly, warning me not to as well. Some people like to take their time before getting another dog, after losing one, and they shouldn't be pushed into it.

But Mrs. Goldmeyer sees me sitting in the waiting room, and even though she is still sniffling, she stops by to say hello. "What have we here?" she asks.

I tell her I'm trying to find the puppy a home, that her owners didn't want to pay to have her leg fixed. But I'm careful to not make it seem as though I'm asking her to take the dog.

"What's her name?" Mrs. Goldmeyer dabs at her eyes with her wadded tissue.

"She doesn't have a name yet," I say. "Her owners only had her a week and hadn't decided on one yet."

"Can I hold her?" Mrs. Goldmeyer asks.

I nod. Mrs. Goldmeyer scoops her up, laying a cheek against her soft ear. The pup makes a content whimpering noise.

"Her name is Kismet," Mrs. Goldmeyer announces after a few moments. "Do you know what Kismet means?" she asks.

"No," I say.

"It means fate. And I think I'd like to take her home with me."

"She's not housebroken yet," I say.

"Well, I've got the summer off, so we'll have plenty of time to work on that."

Before I go to bed that night, I check on my pumpkin plant. The word Mrs. Goldmeyer taught me pops into my head. *Kismet*. I wonder what lies in store for my pumpkin plant. And me? I wish I knew.

Chapter 21

By mid-July I have nine pumpkins of various sizes and shapes set and growing, but my world is falling apart. Right before my eyes. Just after Shirley left and Daddy was done for the day, Aunt Arlene had to come bustling into the office. And now the waiting area is filled with yelling.

"She's going!" Aunt Arlene says.

"No, I'm not!" I say, and I'm stamping my foot like a two-year-old.

"The girl doesn't want to go." Daddy is trying to remain calm, but I'm so angry I can hardly see straight.

Aunt Arlene starts in on one of her long-winded lectures. Words pouring out, and there's no room to stop them.

"Listen, Mother and Father are coming to Ohio for only *one* week this year. Then I'm taking them to visit Aunt Lois in West Virginia; Mother wants to see her sister. Mildred should come along. She doesn't get to see her grandparents that much, and this would allow her to spend more time with them since their visit here will be shorter than usual. Besides, when is the last time she saw her great-aunt Lois? The funeral? Mildred has no cousins, and Aunt Lois has two grandchildren about her age. She should get to know them."

"I don't know," Daddy says slowly. "She has her pumpkins to take care of."

"I understand, and I'm sorry about that. Truly I am. I know how much Mildred cares about those pumpkins. But family is more important. Mother hasn't seen her sister for years, and I think it would mean a lot to her if Mildred could come with us. I don't think I'm asking too much. It's not as if I'm trying to torture the girl."

Daddy sighs and rubs the back of his head, further messing up his already messy hair. "Mildred, it's only for a week. I can help take care of your pumpkins. I bet Jacob would be willing to help, too." He locks eyes with me. "It's not against the rules to have a little help. Everything will be okay. I promise."

I don't say anything. I just glare at Aunt Arlene and head outside to check on my pumpkins.

As the door slams behind me, I can hear Aunt Arlene telling Daddy how the trip will be good for me.

But it won't be. Not for me. And definitely not for my pumpkins.

Chapter 22

I've been moping around for the past two days, but now I have to get my mind clear and concentrate. Time for culling.

Today I will eliminate—cut off—the weakest-looking pumpkin. I will gradually repeat this process over the next couple of weeks until I am left with, I hope, the best one. Culling is important because it means more nutrients and better growth for those that remain. If I left every pumpkin on the vine, they would never reach their maximum size.

My pumpkins now range in size from slightly

bigger than a basketball to about half that size. I can't help remembering my third growing season, when my pumpkins were at this stage.

It was two years ago, and I had such a good feeling about the way things were going. I had finally realized "special powers" had nothing to do with success. So I got online and read everything I could about growing pumpkins before I started my seed. I had also read several editions of *How-to-Grow World Class Giant Pumpkins*, by Don Langevin. I knew it would be complicated. I knew it would be hard. But I had knowledge, and that counted for a lot.

Then there I was at Aunt Arlene's for her Sunday dinner, when all of a sudden balls of ice started plinking against the dining room window. Despite Aunt Arlene's protests, Daddy and I ran straight to his truck and gunned it for home. But we were too late; there was nothing we could do. The pumpkins were pitted from hail. Daddy's truck didn't look too good either; he had to take it to the shop to repair the dents. Aunt Arlene said he was crazy for driving it in a hailstorm, but he said it would have gotten damaged anyway by sitting in her driveway while we had dinner.

Anyway, I tried my best to care for my hurt pumpkins, but the injury to their skins eventually caused black rot. Let's just say it's not a pretty way for a pumpkin to go.

The week after they turned to ugly dark mush, Grover Fernhart had stopped by Daddy's office to get a rabies shot for his border collie. I happened to be hanging out, helping at the front desk. Of course, Grover had to go and ask how my pumpkins were doing.

I hung my head and stared at the floor. "Black rot. From the hailstorm."

"Well, that's too bad," he said. "The hailstorm didn't reach my part of Pickaway County, fortunately."

I couldn't even bear to look at Grover's *fortunate* face. But he only came in seventh that year at the Pumpkin Show, so I felt some sense of satisfaction.

I've got my hands on my hips, looking over my nine baby pumpkins, when I hear bicycle wheels rolling up behind me.

It's Jacob.

He sees the sharp knife I placed on the ground. "Which one?" he asks.

I have already decided which one to cull, but I ask Jacob to guess. I'm fully expecting him to pick out the smallest one, but he surprises me.

"That one there," he points to the third smallest.

"Why?"

"The stem's way too short and stunted. Also, it's not growing on the outside of the vine curve. You'd have to reposition it big time. It doesn't have a chance."

I wipe at sweat forming on my forehead; it's humid already this morning. "See you've learned a thing or two." I reach down for the knife, march over, and lop the poor pumpkin off its vine. I feel a little tinge of guilt for doing so. Like I'm being mean somehow. But I know it's absolutely necessary if I want to compete come the third Wednesday of October.

Chapter 23

Done with my first culling, Jacob and I head back to the house to grab a couple of cold cans of root beer. We sit on the porch, taking swigs, and I tell him about the gosh-awful trip I have to make with Aunt Arlene, Grandma Mildred, and Grandpa Owen to West Virginia.

"I can't believe your dad is making you go," he says.

"I know. Usually we do as we please, but every once in a while Aunt Arlene gets to him, and he can't say no."

"Maybe you'll be lucky and come down with a terrible stomach virus the day you have to leave." Jacob laughs. "Then no one will make you go."

"You don't know Aunt Arlene that well. I'd still have to go," I tell him. But I allow myself to imagine a long car trip where I am constantly throwing up on poor Aunt Arlene. It makes me feel a little better.

Jacob downs his last bit of root beer and nudges me. "I'll do what I can to help while you're gone. I've been watching you long enough to know a lot about pumpkin growing. I knew which one to cull today, didn't I?"

"Yes, you did." I set down my can of root beer and hunch over, putting my elbows on my knees. "Thanks. Dad said you would help. And he said he would, too."

I know that in the best interest of my pumpkin plant I am going to have to let someone else watch over it while I'm gone. But I'm sure no one could do a better job than I could. My whole trip is going to be spent in worry.

We bring the chessboard out to the porch and play a game. This time it takes Jacob nearly an hour to beat me. And he never once has to shake his head at me for making an illegal move. I'm proud of myself. And I can tell Jacob is proud of me, too. He's grinning—not because he won but because I played well.

Even from the shade of the porch I notice the sun is beating down superhard. So after Jacob leaves, I pound in and secure stakes in the ground around each pumpkin. I attach squares of cloth to the tops of the stakes. This will provide protection. The harsh heat and sun of mid-to-late summer can be harmful to giant pumpkins, causing cracks in the skin. When I am eventually left with my final pumpkin, I will then have one large tarp for shade protection.

My vines have sprawled quite a bit, so I go to the garage to get a pile of boards I purchased from the lumber company. I use them to create common walking paths around the vines. This will prevent soil from compacting as I continue to care for my stretching plant. I am containing the growth, though, by pruning and training vines into what is called a Christmas tree pattern, my plant taking on the shape of a big triangle.

I remember Grover Fernhart once saying that taking care of these giant pumpkins was like taking care of a baby. He's wrong. It's like taking care of a whole passel of babies. Then you pick out a favorite and spoil it rotten, selflessly catering to its every need no matter what. But I'm not complaining.

Chapter 24

I get up early, as usual, and head outside while there is still dew on the grass and it's barely light. I've been helping Daddy out in his office a lot this summer in between tending to my pumpkins, but today Jacob's parents are taking him and me to play putt-putt golf in Columbus.

I do my watering, fertilizing, pruning, weeding, checking for bugs, and daily measuring of each pumpkin's circumference with a measuring tape. I am now keeping a diary of growth. It will help me ultimately decide which pumpkin is the last survivor of the patch. It's been a little over a week since I culled my first pumpkin. Now three more have bit the dust, so I have five nice prospects left. Several are very big for this early in the season. As I stare at them, my heart swells with hope.

Mr. and Mrs. Buckner settle into a shaded patio table overlooking the maze of green with its wind-mills, castles, and caves. Jacob and I take our clubs and balls. He chose a green ball. I chose an orange one, of course. It is a pleasant summer day. Some clouds, but sunshine peeking in and out.

Halfway through, on hole nine, Jacob and I are each three over par. Both of us acting like we are determined to beat the other. It's fun to pretend that winning really means something. Of course it doesn't matter a hill of beans.

On the last hole Jacob messes up, taking five strokes. But I get a hole in one, sealing my championship. I let out a whoop, and Jacob pretends to stab himself in the heart. Then all at once our pleasant day turns rainy.

We dash inside, return our clubs, and find Jacob's parents in the food court. They ordered a large pizza earlier, and it is ready just in time. We sit at a table, while watching the weather grow worse as we eat lunch. Rain coming down hard.

"Guess you might not have to worry about watering pumpkins in the morning," Jacob says.

I nod, mouth stuffed with pepperoni pizza. Sometimes it's nice to have a little break.

By the time we head out to the car, thunder is rumbling and lightning is flashing.

Forty minutes later we are close to home, listening to the radio, when there's an announcement. A serious male voice says a tornado watch has been issued for Pickaway County until six o'clock.

"Oh my," says Mrs. Buckner.

"It's just a watch, not a warning," Mr. Buckner says. "Nothing to fret about. Yet."

Suddenly I can't stop the image of my five pumpkins being picked up in the air and tossed, smashed on the ground miles away from their patch.

The scene appears over and over in my head like a hiccup.

I mean, Daddy and I can seek shelter in the cellar. But my pumpkins? Nothing could protect them from a tornado. Nothing.

"You're thinking about your pumpkins, aren't you?" Jacob asks. I can tell he is worried about them too.

I nod, and the two of us are quiet the rest of the way home.

Chapter 25

I spend the next few hours looking out the kitchen window that faces our backyard. While I am scanning the horizon for a dark spiral in the sky, Arnold is hovering around my feet, whimpering. He hates storms. But Wilber is sleeping peacefully, sprawled out on a warm rug near the kitchen sink.

Daddy closes his office at one o'clock on Saturdays, so he is in the living room watching TV. Some news show. I hear mumbling reporter voices.

I have no idea why I am obsessively looking out the window, as there is no way I could stop a tornado from destroying my pumpkins. But somehow it makes me feel better to keep watch over them.

From the living room comes a high-pitched tone. The emergency warning system. I run to the side of the chair Daddy's sitting in. The words scrolling at the bottom of the TV screen state that a tornado has been sighted in Pickaway County. All viewers in the area are advised to seek shelter.

"Guess it's time to head for the cellar." Daddy jumps up, and I follow him as he runs to the kitchen and grabs a flashlight and battery-powered radio from a drawer. I pick up a still-whimpering Arnold, Daddy grabs Wilber by his collar, and within seconds we are in the dark, dank cellar of our old farmhouse.

"I have a few animals up in the clinic," Daddy says. "I'm going to get them real quick. The wind is strong, but not horrible here; maybe the tornado was sighted in another part of the county."

"I'll help," I say.

"No, I think I can get them in one trip. Stay here."

The second Daddy leaves I can hear the wind pick up. I wonder how fast tornadoes travel. Could one make it from another part of the county to here in seconds? Minutes? How many miles can they travel? All of a sudden I'm not just worrying about my pumpkins.

It seems like an eternity until Daddy gets back. He's got a cat in a cat carrier and three dogs on leashes. One of them, a tiny Pekingese with a pink bow on the top of her head, starts baring her teeth and growling at the other dogs. She sounds like she wants to eat them alive. Daddy finds a large empty box and gently places her inside. She begins to yap angrily.

"Sorry," Daddy tells her. "Can't have a dogfight on my hands. And though you don't appear to think so, you'd probably be the one in the worst shape if there were a fight. Just doing this for your own good."

With the other dogs out of sight, the Pekingese finally settles down. Daddy's other doggy patients and our own dogs are busy sniffing one another. Arnold is distracted enough by his new company to stop whimpering.

Daddy and I huddle near the flashlight and listen to the radio. Soon I'm back to worrying about my pumpkin patch. Scenes of gooey, slimy pumpkin guts roll around in my head.

Before long the wind dies down, and we find out the tornado did indeed touch down fairly far from us, about twenty miles away. There are reports of trees uprooted and parts of barn and house roofs blown off, but no serious damage or injuries.

"Well, we've had enough excitement for one day," Daddy says. "I think it's safe to go up now."

While Daddy puts the visiting cat and dogs away, I pick up Arnold and grab Wilber's collar, take them upstairs, then run out like crazy to check on my pumpkins. Even though we did not have a tornado, the wind could have been strong enough to do damage to my vines. But I see everything is okay. I still feel faint, though, from all the worrying I did.

By the time Daddy and I sit down to eat, the sky has cleared and looks a strange orange-pink. A thought occurs: a guilty hope that perhaps the tornado has helped me out in my quest to have the biggest pumpkin at the Pumpkin Show.

I swallow a bite of hamburger. "Daddy," I say carefully, "that tornado, any chance it could have hit Grover Fernhart's farm?"

Daddy gives me a pointed look, letting me know he knows exactly what I'm thinking. "No. It was a little closer to him than us, but I doubt his pumpkins were hurt any."

"Oh," I say innocently, "that's good. I was quite worried."

Daddy bursts out laughing. "Yes, Mildred, I bet you were."

Chapter 26

Late next afternoon finds me at the Columbus airport. Aunt Arlene, Uncle Jerald, Daddy, and I are waiting on the arrival of Grandma Mildred and Grandpa Owen. I have this sinking feeling I can't shake. Not because I'm not happy to see my grandparents. I am. But because I know their arrival means I will be leaving for West Virginia in exactly one week. So far, far away from my pumpkin plant.

Soon passengers on my grandparents' flight start filing into the wide hallway. Aunt Arlene is craning her neck and suddenly begins waving. I spy

Grandma and Grandpa, and they spy us as well. Both break into big smiles and hurry toward us. Grandma is wearing a turquoise dress made of stretchy material. It looks nice with her gray, bobbed hair. Grandpa is wearing stretchy-looking clothes too, but not in turquoise, of course. I know some kids have grandparents who look young and dress in jeans, but I have the old-fashioned kind. I like it that way actually.

Grandma hugs me first. I take in the smell of her old-lady perfume. "Oh, my, Mildred," she says. "I've missed you so!" She kisses me on the cheek, wipes off the dark pink lipstick she left, then looks me over good. "Oh, you've got your ears pierced! I just can't believe how you're growing up!"

Grandpa is waiting to give me a hug next, as soon as Grandma is done. His mustache tickles my cheek, and he smells like licorice, his favorite candy.

"How's the pumpkin growing coming along this year?" Grandpa asks as he straightens up.

"Very well, thanks," I say.

"Oh, and we are so excited you are coming with us to visit my sister," Grandma says.

I manage a weak smile.

Aunt Arlene looks pleased as punch.

We eat dinner out. So as soon as we get back home, I excuse myself, saying I have to put my pumpkins to bed. Which is true. I actually place blankets on them at night.

Grandma tells me she would like to see them, but since it's dark outside, she couldn't get a good look anyway, and besides, she is tired from the trip and needs to turn in for the night. "I'd sure like to see them in the morning, though," she says, yawning.

"Sure. Great," I say.

The next morning both Grandma and Grandpa are up at the crack of dawn, so we all go out to inspect my patch. My pumpkins are much bigger than a basketball now. About beach ball size. It's amazing, giant pumpkins can grow ten to twenty pounds in a day, easy. A piece of cake. But what you really strive for is a champ that can put on thirty to forty pounds a day during peak season.

"Five of them . . . my, my," says Grandpa.

"I'll be cutting one of them off tomorrow," I say.

"Oh, isn't that sad," says Grandma.

We went through the same routine last year, me explaining the need to cull and Grandma saying it's sad. But I don't mind. It's nice to have somebody interested in my pumpkins.

"Hey!" says Grandpa. "The one that you cut off—we should take it on our trip. Show it to your great-aunt Lois!"

I imagine Aunt Arlene's face when we load a seventy-five- to a hundred-pound pumpkin into the trunk of her car.

"Good idea," I say.

The next day I have an audience as I decide which pumpkin to cull. I've got my daily growth diary with me, and my grandparents are asking lots of questions.

"This one right here." I point at the third-smallest one. "It's growing at the fastest rate, putting on the most weight this past week. No way will I get rid of that one. It's not the largest right now, but it could very well end up overtaking the biggest two."

"So, biggest isn't always best?" Grandpa has his hand to his chin, and he looks real serious.

"Right. See the smallest? Early on it was bigger than the one I just pointed out. But it has kind of putted along lately. Also, it doesn't have a nice round shape, which is what you'd look for at this stage. And it's not positioned well either. I think its time has come."

As I cut the pumpkin from the vine, it occurs to me how much I like having my grandparents around. I'm old enough that we can have real conversations now. I mean, we talked when I was younger, but it somehow seems different now.

Grandpa offers to carry the culled pumpkin.

"Are you sure? It's heavy. I can just ask Daddy to come out when he has time."

"Nonsense." Grandpa draws himself up tall. "I swim laps every day in Florida. Great shape for my age." He thumps his flat tummy.

I step aside and watch as he walks down the board path to the pumpkin. He strains a bit to lift it and walks slowly, clutching it to his body. "Where do you want it?" he asks, panting.

"Just place it near the cellar door. I'll put it down there, where it's cool, to keep after I wash it off."

Grandpa struggles but places it where I ask. "Let us know if you have a pumpkin headed for the weigh-in this year," he says, still breathing hard. "Maybe we can fly in."

"I will."

"I wish your mother were here to see you growing these pumpkins," Grandma says. "I know how she liked them. She always looked forward to the Pumpkin Show, you know."

"Yes, I know," I say, kind of quietly, and my throat begins to feel like I just swallowed something prickly. My eyes start to get watery, but I don't cry.

Grandpa puts his arm around my shoulder. "I'm surprised you're actually going to West Virginia with us. Will your pumpkins be okay?" he asks.

"Yes, I've been wondering about that . . ." Grandma says, her voice trailing off.

I shrug and focus on the ground. "Daddy said he'll look after them. My friend Jacob, too." I don't tell them Aunt Arlene is forcing me to go. I know the two of them are looking forward to having me along for the trip, and I don't have the heart to tell them I would rather stay home. Besides, there's no way Aunt Arlene would ever relent and change her mind. That much I know for sure.

Chapter 27

August 1. I'll be leaving for West Virginia around noon to visit Great-Aunt Lois and Great-Uncle Harry. Unfortunately I have not come down with a stomach virus as I hoped, so I will not be throwing up on Aunt Arlene. I am sorely disappointed.

I study the three remaining pumpkins I have left. I have a big decision to make. Should I cut one or two? There are contradictory theories among giant-pumpkin growers. Some say to let one remain on the vine, that that's the only way it will reach maximum growth. Others swear a Howard Dill plant has the strength and energy to easily handle two, maybe even three. What to do?

Last year was my best season ever. I had decided to cull down to one. I was pleased with the results. I estimated my giant was about six hundred pounds. Not big enough to win, certainly, but big enough to weigh in and display for all to see. The only problem was a dill ring, an indented line around the circumference, had shown up. I knew it indicated a weakness in the interior wall, but I had come this far with it, and otherwise it was in good shape. I had seen others with dill rings displayed in the past. It was a common but not necessarily fatal problem.

We gathered a crew to help with the loading: Jacob, his dad, Daddy, and four of his friends, one who owned a truck with a flatbed trailer he was letting us borrow. I stood back to supervise as everyone else found a place around a tarp with hand holes, specially made for lifting giant pumpkins, that Daddy had bought for my birthday. All went well with lifting it into the air. It was glorious, the fall morning sun hitting pale orange skin. Then it was shuffled over and slowly placed onto the trailer. There was a small thud from the impact. And my giant split wide open. Daddy, who never cusses, said a cussword, and then we were all silent at the horror of what had just happened.

It did not make it to the Pumpkin Show, displayed for all to see.

The memory still stings. It stings enough that I am able to make my decision. I'm going to cull just one more. Two will remain. I pray it's the right decision.

I study my growth diary and look the three over for all strengths and weaknesses. I make my choice: the second largest will go. I pray this is the right decision as well.

Based on measurements the one I cut off is probably a little over two hundred pounds. It's Sunday and Daddy's not working, so I'll go ask him and Grandpa to move it for me with the lifting tarp.

When it is all set to go, Daddy asks where I want it.

"Put it near the driveway, by the garage, for now," I say. The garage is in back of our office addition.

"For now? Do you mean I have to move this thing twice?" Daddy doesn't sound pleased.

"Later it can go in the field to rot."

"Why can't I just put it in the field now?" he asks.

"I have plans for it. Just wait, you'll see."

Jacob stops by to see me off. I give both him and Daddy four pages of typed instructions on what to do while I'm gone. We eat a lunch of soup and sandwiches with Grandpa and Grandma, and just as we finish, Aunt Arlene shows up.

The luggage is brought out to the driveway. Wilber and Arnold slip out the door and are running circles around everyone. They know something is up. I give them each a hug good-bye before Daddy herds them back into the house. Aunt Arlene opens the trunk and reaches for one of the suitcases lined up beside her car.

"The pumpkin," I whisper to Grandpa.

"Oh, yes. Save room for the pumpkin," Grandpa tells her.

Aunt Arlene gets this crazed look, which she directs at me. I stand by the big two-hundred-pound pumpkin that was culled this morning and look down at it, causing Aunt Arlene all of a sudden to notice it too.

"What? We can't take that! The trunk door will never close around it. There will be no room for our luggage!" Aunt Arlene is aghast.

Jacob is standing next to me, and his shoulders start shaking and he puts his hand to his mouth. I can tell he is trying hard not to laugh.

I let Aunt Arlene stew for a few seconds, then innocently say, "Not that pumpkin."

Jacob breaks down and starts laughing. Me too. Even Grandma and Grandpa are grinning. Aunt Arlene pretends to ignore us, and I send Daddy to the cellar to get the smaller one I kept.

Aunt Arlene allows the smaller one to be loaded

into the car, along with all our bags. But she still doesn't look too happy about it.

Daddy shakes his head at me, then hugs me good-bye.

And it occurs to me that leaving him will hurt just as much as leaving those two pumpkins, still growing on the vine.

Chapter 28

We arrive at Aunt Lois's a little after five. She lives in a small, well-kept, one-story house. Cute front porch. Tidy landscaping. Grandpa jumps out of the car and opens the trunk. First thing he heaves out happens to be my pumpkin.

Aunt Arlene purses her lips but says nothing.

Grandpa waddles over to the front porch, where he places my pumpkin, then trots back. By now Aunt Arlene, Grandma, and I have our suitcases in hand. Grandpa gets his, and before we can ring the doorbell, Aunt Lois is flapping around, ushering us into the house.

"Mildred! My, how you've changed!" Aunt Lois's hand flutters to her cheek, as if she is surprised.

Of course I've changed; it has been years since she has seen me. But I smile in reply.

Aunt Lois's husband, Uncle Harry, is shaking hands with Grandpa. "It's been a long time," he says.

I notice he does not mention how much Grandpa has changed.

Soon we are shown to our rooms. Aunt Arlene is put in a spare bedroom, and Grandma and Grandpa are too. There isn't a spare bedroom for me, but I am more than happy. I have a couch in a small office off the living room. To keep me company is a small TV and computer. Yeah!

"Feel free to use the computer to chat with your friends if you want," Aunt Lois tells me.

"Thanks." I can't believe my good luck. I can keep track of the weather!

I am left alone to settle in. I turn on the TV and

find The Weather Channel. Then I look up the weather forecast for Circleville on the computer. Doesn't hurt to have two sources. Maybe it will ease my worries, just a little, to know how much sun and rain my twin pumpkins are getting.

All at once Grandpa is calling for me to come out of my room. He leads everyone out to the porch to show off my pumpkin. He is telling Aunt Lois and Uncle Harry all about how I am going to have the biggest pumpkin at the Pumpkin Show. "This is one of the rejects," he says, "but isn't it a nice one?"

"Sure is." Aunt Lois nods. "I could make some nice pies with it."

"Oh, you can't do that. They aren't good for eating," I explain. "And all the stuff we use to grow them—it wouldn't be safe to make pies from anyway."

Aunt Lois and Uncle Harry start asking lots of questions.

I'm enjoying all this talk about giant-pumpkin growing, but Aunt Arlene has to ruin it by interrupting the conversation. "It is very stressful for Mildred. Just occupies all her time. I thought a little break, here in West Virginia, would do her good. Now, when will your grandchildren be coming over?"

"Tyson and Amanda will be coming tomorrow afternoon," Aunt Lois says.

"Good. Didn't you say dinner was close to being finished?" Aunt Arlene continues. "Maybe we should go on inside."

"Oh, heavens, yes! Don't want anything overdone!" Aunt Lois scurries inside, and we all follow.

We are all seated at the dining room table, and Aunt Lois is rushing around, placing dishes heaped with steaming food in front of us. I notice she is the type of grandma that wears jeans and colors her hair. I know she is only a few years younger than

Grandma Mildred, but she looks and acts much younger than that. She leans in close to pour ice tea in my glass. She smells younger too.

I eat pork chops with some kind of glaze. Stuffing and rolls. Salad with homemade dressing. There is chocolate cream pie for dessert. Even though I am missing my pumpkins, the food tastes too good once I start, and I can't help stuffing myself until I'm half miserable. Eating food like this is a comfort too, I guess.

I figure Aunt Arlene must have inherited her cooking genes from Aunt Lois. Daddy and I have gone to Grandma and Grandpa's in Florida for Christmas a couple of times. We always end up eating out at restaurants. It's funny, my grandma looks like the type that would cook and doesn't, while Aunt Lois doesn't but does.

I say I'm tired after dinner and head for my office room. I know that weather in Ohio can change unexpectedly and fast, so I check the computer again.

Everything looks fine. I fall asleep an hour later, listening to The Weather Channel.

I wake up in the middle of the night, my heart thumping at my chest. Awful dreams. Terrible dreams. Swirls of hailstorms and tornadoes and me fighting off giant pumpkin-eating insects the size of Aunt Arlene.

Chapter 29

I spend the morning hanging around the living room, listening to all the older people talk. But I manage to sneak into my office room every thirty minutes or so to check the weather. It's the only thing I can do right now, so far away, to somehow care for my pumpkins. I find comfort in it. I know I can call Daddy to tell him to change my instructions if need be. I miss getting up in the morning and seeing how much bigger they got. I know they will look so different when I get home.

Around two o'clock my comfortable schedule

changes. Aunt Lois's daughter and her children arrive. I am introduced to Tyson and Amanda.

Tyson looks to be about fifteen. He has long brown hair that hangs in his eyes. I can tell he isn't thrilled to be here.

Amanda, who is a year older than I am, is very pretty. Tan and blond. She is dressed in a pink sleeveless blouse and white shorts. Aunt Arlene is eyeing her as though she approves. Like she will be a good role model for me.

The grown-ups talk, and we kids sit around feeling awkward. Finally Amanda looks at me and says, "Want to go for a walk? I'll show you around."

I really don't. How can I check on the weather in Circleville? I like having an accurate image of my plant in my head. Last I checked it was partly cloudy, so I'm imagining sun dappling here and there over big green leaves and two orange pumpkins. If it starts to rain I want to know, so the picture in my mind can change.

Before I can answer Amanda, Aunt Arlene says, "Yes! A walk! That would be nice!"

I follow Amanda out the front door, while Tyson tags along behind us.

We have barely started walking down the sidewalk when Tyson ditches us. "Nice meeting you, Mildred." He gives a friendly wave good-bye. "I'm going to meet Justin at the park to play some ball," he tells his sister.

"Good riddance anyway." Amanda smirks. "He is so *annoying*. All the time looking at himself in the mirror. He is in love with Darla Carson. He's probably meeting her at the park. My parents don't approve."

"Why not?" I ask.

"Because she wears her shorts too high and her shirts too low." She leans closer and whispers, "She's got stuff spilling out of her clothes that shouldn't be spilling out."

"Oh."

"So what do you do for fun?" she asks.

I wonder if I should tell her. I decide to go ahead, as it is easier than making something up. "I grow giant pumpkins," I say, like it is no big deal.

"Was that yours on Grandma Lois's front porch? I saw one there. It's big, bigger than the ones I usually see around Halloween. But not by much. Doesn't look like a giant one to me." She realizes what she said did not come out right and puts her hand to her mouth. "Sorry . . ."

"Oh, that one I cut off early," I explain. "I've got two growing right now. By the time I'm done they'll be monsters. I'm hoping over a thousand pounds."

"Really?" Amanda stops in her tracks. "That's amazing."

"It is?" I stand beside her, surprised.

She slowly starts walking again. "How do you get them that big? Maybe I should grow one."

I shake my head. "It is very complicated. You have to be superdevoted. Lots of hard work." Goodness, I realize I just sounded like Grover Fernhart. So I say, "But if you really want to know . . ."

"I guess I probably wouldn't have time for it." Amanda wrinkles her nose and scrunches her mouth up to one side.

"So, what do you do for fun?" I ask.

"Me? I wrestle."

"What?" Now I am the one stopping in my tracks.

"I pinned three boys last season and lost only one match. Going to a special camp next week, so I'll get even better."

"Isn't that unusual?"

"Look who's talking, giant-pumpkin girl." She laughs.

I laugh too.

"See, my dad was state champ way back when. He always hoped Tyson would wrestle. Follow in his footsteps, you know. But Tyson, well, he never wanted anything to do with it. He likes other sports." Amanda throws a thumb at herself proudly. "So Dad started teaching me and taking me to tournaments."

"Neat." I grin, thinking of how Aunt Arlene is probably so sure that Amanda is a prim and proper young lady because of the way she looks.

"So, you want to go spy on Tyson at the park?" Amanda asks.

"Sure."

I find out that Darla Carson does indeed wear her shorts too short and her shirts too low—with stuff spilling out that shouldn't.

Chapter 30

I spend the week hanging out with Amanda. I haven't told Aunt Arlene yet that she wrestles and likes spying on her brother who is in love with Darla Carson. I think I will save that for the trip home tomorrow; I'm not looking forward to the long drive with only Aunt Arlene for company.

I like Amanda. And she seems to like me too. She told me she would miss me because the girls her age who live nearby are annoying. I think *annoying* must be her favorite word. She uses it all the time. She is the closest thing to a cousin I've got, and I feel fortunate I don't find her annoying. That would have made this trip totally unbearable. Actually we didn't really spend that much time spying on Tyson; it got major boring. So we swam, we climbed trees, we caught crawdads in a nearby creek, we talked. We even played chess and were pretty evenly matched. Sometimes she would win; sometimes I would. Amanda said maybe she will come visit next summer if she can, so she can see how giant pumpkins are grown.

It was hard saying good-bye to Grandma and Grandpa earlier this evening. We saw them off at the airport in Charleston, the city closest to the small town we are in. They are flying into Atlanta, then on to Florida. Right before they left both of them squeezed me so hard it nearly hurt. But I didn't mind.

"You take care of those pumpkins now," Grandpa called out as he walked away. "Make me proud come the Pumpkin Show."

For some stupid reason I got a little teary-eyed,

but I managed not to cry, which would have been embarrassing.

And I have to say, Aunt Lois and Uncle Harry have been nothing but nice. But I really can't wait to get back to Daddy and my pumpkins. I checked the weather whenever I could this past week, and there were no surprises. My pumpkins had almost perfect conditions for putting on weight. Daddy called a couple of times to ask how I was doing and to reassure me everything was fine. Still, I won't feel okay until I can see for myself. And I feel awful guilty that Daddy and Jacob are doing all *my* work. Doesn't seem right.

I settle into the office couch, pulling the blanket up to my chin. Tomorrow just can't come quick enough.

We are about thirty minutes from home when I say to Aunt Arlene, "Do you know Amanda wrestles?"

"What?"

"She wrestles boys. Pins them." I let my eyes

grow wide with excitement. "Maybe I'll wrestle on a team when I get to junior high."

Aunt Arlene is speechless.

I really have no interest in wrestling, but I do enjoy teasing her like this, so I get a few more jabs in. "And Tyson has a girlfriend. She wears her shorts too short, and her shirts are too low—she's practically bursting out of them. And they sure kiss an awful lot."

"Oh my." Aunt Arlene frowns, and her lips are tight.

I can tell she is thinking taking me on this trip might not have been such a good idea after all. I know I'm being a little mean, but it serves her right. She took me away from what I love. And that's hard to forgive. Even if I did have a sort of enjoyable time.

First thing I do when Aunt Arlene parks the car in our driveway is jump out and sprint to the pumpkin patch. My two pumpkins look huge. Beanbag chair size. I'm guessing they've put on at least another two hundred pounds since I've been gone, doubling their weight. Suddenly I get goose bumps, picturing Jacob and Daddy watering, fertilizing, weeding, and measuring. I thought it would be terrible having someone else do those things. But it makes me feel good, knowing that someone else cares about my pumpkins too.

As soon as I step inside, Daddy's arms are there to hug me. Arnold and Wilber are dancing around, jumping, they are so excited to see me.

And I feel a bit like Dorothy from *The Wizard of Oz*. There really is no place like home.

Chapter 31

Three weeks after getting back from West Virginia, and school is already in full swing. Mrs. Kimble, my sixth-grade teacher, is standing in front of the class, assigning a major project.

"You are to write a two- to three-page paper on someone who is important to you," she says, "someone you admire, someone who inspires you. It must be someone you have never met but would like to meet. Due on Monday. Be prepared to give an oral report."

I don't have to think long to know who I am

doing my paper on. Howard Dill, of course.

It was hard returning to school come the end of August, leaving my pumpkins for a good portion of the day, but not as hard as leaving them for a whole week like I did when Aunt Arlene dragged me to West Virginia.

My two pumpkins are so whoppin' big right now. To get the most accurate weight estimate possible, I am using the "over the top" method, which combines three measurements: circumference, side to side, and stem to blossom, all added together. One pumpkin measures 366 combined inches. That's about 1,027 pounds, according to the chart I use. The other is 371 inches, about 1,069 pounds.

The Pumpkin Show is almost seven weeks away. And even though their growth rate will be slowing down as they mature, there is still plenty of time for my pumpkins to put on even more weight. I'm trying not to get my hopes up too much, though. Something always ends up going wrong, it seems. But I do have a good chance, I think, of not only finally having a pumpkin displayed in the middle of town for all to see, but of winning.

The bell rings, and it's time for recess. It's not as much fun as last year, though. Jacob is in junior high now, so I no longer have him to keep me company. But Aunt Arlene took me shopping for school clothes, which means I'm dressed nice enough for the other girls to treat me okay.

Gloria Mathis ends up cornering me by the monkey bars. "I hear you are going to win biggest pumpkin this year," she says.

"Who told you that?" I ask. I haven't bothered talking to the girls in my class about pumpkins since I first tried back in second grade and they found Gloria's fingernail polish more interesting.

"My mother knows your aunt Arlene," says Gloria.

"Are you saying my aunt Arlene told your mother?" I ask.

"Yes."

"Oh." I find this hard to believe.

"So are you?" Gloria asks. "Are you going to win?"

I shrug my shoulders.

"The winner gets a check for two thousand dollars. And a trophy almost as tall as a man," Gloria explains to a few other girls standing around.

"Two thousand dollars!" Alicia Weber says, dropping her jaw.

Again I shrug. The money would be nice. And the trophy, too. But it really isn't why I'm a giant-pumpkin grower.

After school I do what I always do when coming home. I check on my pumpkins. I'm admiring the larger one. Most people wouldn't think it's beautiful. Rough, bumpy skin, flat on the bottom now so it's not perfectly round; skin a faint pinkish orangish gray, not bright like jack-o'-lanterns have; stem sticking out on the side, not the top. But to me it looks like a champion. Perfect for a giant. Suddenly I stop cold. A pitiful whimper escapes my mouth.

A crack. I see a fresh crack at the top, near the stem. Jellylike sap is oozing out.

A "Hey!" comes from behind.

I turn around and see Jacob approaching. He gets a little closer and sees the expression on my face. "What's wrong?"

I point to the crack and start to cry.

Chapter 32

Jacob follows me as I run to the house. I grab my toothbrush from the bathroom drawer, dash to the garage, rummage through a large cupboard where I keep some of my supplies, and quickly find a fungicide solution. Within seconds I'm brushing away the gooey sap leaking out of the crack with my soft toothbrush. I clean the area with water. I wait for it to dry, then treat the crack with the fungicide.

"Think it will be okay?" Jacob asks.

"Maybe. I'm really going to have to baby it. If

the crack grows and breaks through the skin to the interior and air gets in, it's a goner."

"Oh." Jacob looks concerned. "Talk about terrible."

"Believe me, I'll be praying up a storm it doesn't happen."

I tell Daddy, as the two of us are fixing dinner, that I need a new toothbrush.

"Why?" he asks.

"Had to use it to clean a crack."

"Which pumpkin?"

I let out a long sigh. "The bigger one."

I spend the weekend tending to my injured pumpkin and working on my paper for Mrs. Kimble. I know a lot of kids, when they are given a page range, always end up with the least required. But I'm having a hard time limiting my paper on Howard. Dill to three pages.

On Monday morning, before I even eat breakfast or shower, I walk the boards around long full vines to get a good look at the crack that has been haunting me. It's bigger, deeper, and sap once again is bubbling up. I clean it again with my toothbrush and water. I do my watering and fertilizing, then get ready for school. Before I leave, I seal up the crack with grafting wax and say a little prayer that this will do the trick. The thought of losing this one makes me physically ill.

Gloria Mathis is standing in front of the class, talking about the teenage actor she is still in love with. This is her important person? The one who inspires her? The one she wants to meet? I believe the only reason he is important to her is that she wants to date and marry him. It makes me want to gag, but considering how nauseated I already feel, that would not be a good idea.

Arnie Bradford is next. His report is about the best player on the Cleveland Cavaliers basketball team. This does make sense. Everyone knows Arnie is crazy about basketball and wants to make the junior high team next year. And everyone knows he will. On the playground he once spent the entire recess shooting baskets without missing a single shot.

Mrs. Kimble calls me up. I know so much about Howard Dill that I don't even need to look at my paper to talk. Of course I mention how he developed the giant pumpkin seed by trial and error over many years and how he broke the world record in 1979. And also how more than three thousand pounds of his patented seeds are sold worldwide every year. But there are lots more interesting things I cover. Like even though he doesn't grow giant pumpkins for competitions anymore, his family still grows two acres of them on his farm in Nova Scotia on a yearly basis. And his farm, which has been in his family for five generations, is also the home of Long Pond, where the game of hockey supposedly originated in Canada in the 1800s.

I wrap up the report by telling my classmates about my two pumpkins and their estimated weights. As I look around at everyone's faces, I can tell they are impressed. When Mrs. Kimble asks if anyone has any questions, lots of hands go up.

A week later I get my paper back. Fifty points for my written report and fifty points for the oral portion. One hundred percent. A+. But it's hard to feel pleased. Several hours ago I had to lop off the bigger pumpkin from the stem. It lost its battle with the crack.

Chapter 33

The day I've been waiting for. Morning of the third Wednesday of October, and a crowd of people is gathered in the backyard: Daddy, his friend with the truck and low flatbed trailer, another friend sitting at the controls of a small track hoe, Jacob and his dad, Grandma and Grandpa, who flew in from Florida, and other curious onlookers Daddy knows. Aunt Arlene is absent, though. I thought maybe even with her hard feelings about the time I spend on my pumpkins, she would be here. I guess I thought wrong. Still, I'm so happy today I'm not going to let it bother me.

A couple of hours ago, when it was barely light outside, I cut my pumpkin from its vine. I washed it with dish detergent mixed with water and used a soft brush to remove dirt. Then I rinsed it with bleach-laced water and buffed it with some old towels.

It's perfect weather now. Low sixties and bright sunshine, hardly any clouds. I don't even miss that pumpkin that I cut off last month, because the other one continued growing at a remarkable pace. It's Goliath. Like a fairy godmother wouldn't have to wave a wand over it to turn it into a carriage. If it was hollowed out and put on its end, Cinderella could easily sit inside—with just enough room for Prince Charming, too. Estimated weight: 1,369 pounds. Of course the true weight won't be found until it's weighed later this morning.

And to think I could have culled this one right before I left for West Virginia. I made the right decision to keep two. I really did need a backup. Don't even want to think how I'd be feeling right now if I had only the one that ended up cracked and ruined.

The backyard wouldn't be full of people at this very moment, that's for sure.

Everyone is in high spirits. Smiling. Laughing. I've been patted on the back about a hundred times the past hour, everyone telling me I've got the winner for sure.

I won't be using the lifting tarp this year; my mammoth pumpkin is just too big for it. I try to shake the image of last year's ruptured pumpkin out of my head as the track hoe, driven by Daddy's friend, slowly eases over. Attached to the arm of the machine is the lifting device I purchased last month in anticipation of this day, a metal ring at the top with five straps hanging down. It is positioned over my pumpkin, and I open the bottom drawstring that connects the straps. I pull the straps over my pumpkin, and once the drawstring is secured beneath, I motion to the track hoe driver and hold my breath as my humongous orange blob is raised into the air. A few minutes later the pumpkin is safely guided and settled onto a big square of Styrofoam padding, which I placed on the flatbed earlier. Everyone starts clapping and cheering. No spilled pumpkin guts!

Daddy, Jacob, and I climb into the truck, and we are on our way.

"Whatever you do," I tell Daddy as the truck creeps from our driveway onto the road, "don't get in a wreck."

Chapter 34

We are in the middle of a long line of trucks on Main Street. I'm so excited I can hardly sit still.

"You and Jacob go check out the competition," Daddy says. "I'll keep watch over the pumpkin."

Jacob and I walk toward the head of the line. I whisper guessed weights as we pass each pumpkin waiting to be weighed. "Three hundred . . . , eight hundred . . . , four hundred . . . , a thousand . . . , four hundred . . . , nine hundred . . . , five hundred . . . oh, dear Lord." I stare at the monster to my right. It's noticeably bigger than mine.

A woman sitting in the driver's seat waves at me. Francine Myers. She won last year. "Nice one, don't you think?" she says.

I nod. Jacob looks as crushed as I feel.

Jacob and I continue walking, but I'm no longer prattling off weights. I'm silent for a while. So is he. Finally he says, "Nothing wrong with second place."

"I guess that would be pretty cool," I say, but without much enthusiasm.

Once we reach the weighing station we turn around and walk the other way. A few minutes later we stop by Daddy, who is leaning his head out the truck window.

I shake my head and scrunch up my face. "I'm not going to win. I saw one that's bigger."

"Bigger isn't always heavier," Daddy says, trying to reassure me.

"I know, but it's a pretty good predictor of the outcome." I try not to sound too disappointed.

"Did you see Grover's pumpkin?" Daddy asks.

"No, guess he must be somewhere behind us in line." I can't help thinking that maybe his will be even bigger than Francine's.

"Maybe we should walk down that way," Jacob says. "Check out the rest of the competition."

I begin to find myself feverishly hoping for second place like Jacob said. I'm here, I remind myself. Never made it this far before. My pumpkin will be displayed in the middle of town for all to see. Isn't that what I've always wanted?

Not a single truck we pass has a pumpkin that can compare with mine or Francine's. I feel my spirits lift.

The very last truck has Grover Fernhart standing beside it, and he's talking to another man. He points to his pumpkin, which is on the smallish side for a giant. "I can't take it anymore," he says. "I swear, this will be my last year. Put my heart and soul into it, over twenty years, and what do I have to show for it? Won't even place this year."

I want to be smug. I want to march right up to Grover and say, "Ha, I grew a bigger one than you." But a bit of sympathy and compassion stirs inside me, and I can't. I know what it is like to be disappointed, and poor Grover has been at it a lot longer than I have.

Chapter 35

At ten o'clock the first pumpkin is weighed at Court and Main. Jacob and I are in the crowd, watching. Daddy is manning the truck, ready to inch it forward as each truck takes a turn.

A forklift with one long, extra-thick post has a lifting device attached to its tip. The metal ring with dangling canvas straps is just like mine at home. Pumpkin Show workers open a drawstring at the bottom of the straps. It makes a wide circle, which they place over the pumpkin. After they cinch it below the pumpkin's bottom curve, the pumpkin is hoisted into the air, letting the connected scale do its work. A digital readout nearby lists the weight, and it's called out to the crowd.

We watch as the process is done over and over again. Pumpkins are delicately moved by the forklift into the display area. Then markers are used to write weights on different shades of pumpkin skin. It takes almost an hour until it is time to weigh Francine's whopper. The crowd murmurs and gasps at the sight. Everyone knows this is it. Once it is lifted in the air there is total silence.

The weight is called out: 1,373 pounds.

Everyone's yelling, whooping. Francine is beaming.

I lean over and whisper to Jacob, "I still might have a chance. Hers wasn't as heavy as it looked."

Chapter 36

An hour after Francine's weigh-in, Daddy pulls up, and I leave Jacob in the crowd to run over to claim the pumpkin behind the truck as mine.

"It's enormous," I hear someone say. "But I don't believe it is as big as that one thousand three hundred seventy-three pounder."

Daddy gets out and stands by me. The straps get cinched around my pumpkin. My heart is going full speed, and I'm not sure I can survive the suspense. I'm afraid I'm going to pass out before I find out what my pumpkin weighs.

Up, up, up it goes.

I stare at the digital readout, and when the numbers flash up, I'm afraid my eyes are playing tricks on me: 1,401 pounds!

When it is announced, all the people lining the intersection of Court and Main go berserk.

I start jumping up and down, screaming my head off. I leap right into Daddy's arms, and he's hugging me tight and jumping up and down, too. Then all at once I'm no longer screaming; I'm sobbing.

Jacob gallops over and Daddy puts me down. I grab Jacob's shoulders and start jumping up and down again, and now I'm no longer sobbing, I'm laughing hysterically.

I know I'm the winner. Everyone knows I'm the winner. Francine comes over and shakes my hand. Even she knows I'm the winner. But there are more pumpkins to weigh before it's official.

I find a place, off to the side, so the next truck can come through, and watch as my pumpkin is placed in the middle of town for all to admire. Its weight confirmed by a thick black marker on its skin.

Grandma and Grandpa soon find me. And someone else pushes through the crowd: Aunt Arlene dragging Uncle Jerald by his arm. "Mildred!" she shouts. "Mildred!" She lets go of Uncle Jerald's arm to give me a hug. "Congratulations!"

"How long have you been here?" I ask.

"Since ten o'clock. You didn't think I would miss the weigh-in, did you?"

I look at her in disbelief.

It's another hour and a half until the last pumpkin is weighed. It belongs to Grover Fernhart. His eyes look tired and sad as his pumpkin is lifted: 680 pounds. Nothing to sneeze at, but Grover just casts his head down, shaking it back and forth. It's his worst showing in years.

Finally the results are announced. And before I know it, I'm holding that two-thousand-dollar check. On my left is a trophy that is taller than I am. On my right is my prizewinning pumpkin.

As cameras are clicking, I look upward, wondering if my mama, way up in heaven, knows what I have done.

A little while later Daddy gives me some spending money and sends me on my way to have fun with Jacob.

First thing I do is head over to the craft stands to buy a set of pumpkin earrings to celebrate my victory. I find a pair to my liking and take out my diamond ones from Aunt Arlene, shoving them deep in the front pocket of my jeans, so they won't get lost. I put in my newly purchased pumpkin ones.

"What do you think?" I ask Jacob.

"Not big enough." He grins.

"Maybe I'll get the weight of mine engraved on each one," I reply.

Next, Jacob and I walk past Lindsey's Bakery and duck inside. The world's largest pumpkin pie is looking smooth and pretty, for now, since it's the first day of the Pumpkin Show. It's so big it looks like they could have used my pumpkin to make it.

Looking at that pie makes us hungry, so we stop at four different food stands, stuffing ourselves silly with junk food.

"Let's go ride some rides," Jacob says.

"Shouldn't we have done that first?" I say, clutching my full stomach.

"Oh, we'll start out easy first. How about the paratroopers? We can save the upside-down ones for later."

And so I find myself, under a purple metal umbrella, flying, feet in the air. It occurs to me I don't feel any different riding this ride. I've been floating on air for the past few hours. I close my eyes and, blissful and full of peace, throw my head back.

Chapter 37

It's Saturday morning, and Daddy is in his office working, while I sit in the waiting room. Jacob and his parents will be picking me up soon to get an early start on the last day of the Pumpkin Show.

On the waiting room coffee table, proudly displayed, is Thursday's *Circleville Herald*. My pumpkin and me on the front page. I've got a huge smile on my face, which is upturned and looking at the sky, as if a plane were flying over and I'm searching for it. I'm hoping maybe Mama knows why.

I've never had more fun at the Pumpkin Show.

I was constantly walking by the giant-pumpkin display. People gathered thick around the chain-link fence, pointing at my pumpkin like it was the most incredible thing they had ever seen.

I heard one mother telling her little girl, "I bet Peter, Peter, Pumpkin Eater could really keep his wife in that one!"

The little girl bobbed her head in agreement, a big smile on her face.

"Maybe I should try to grow one," the mother said.

And with those words I felt as if it was me there with my mama. The memory was so clear I felt like I could reach out and touch Mama's arm. . . .

Suddenly Daddy's office door flies open. Aunt Arlene comes storming in. "Where's my brother?" she asks Shirley, all upset-like.

"Running some tests in the back."

"I need to see him."

Seconds later Daddy is at the front desk, with a bewildered Shirley by his side.

Aunt Arlene's face is flushed red. "Do you know what I heard Grover Fernhart is doing? He is going all over town telling people that Mildred did not grow that pumpkin. He's saying you did it. That Mildred's name was attached for the publicity it would generate, since she's so young. He's saying there is no way a child could produce a winner. I think you should get him on the phone right now, so you can set him straight."

Daddy looks at me. "You want me to call him?"

I think for a moment and shake my head. "No. I think he just feels real bad about losing. Let him be. I know I grew it, and that's what counts. And you did help—"

"One week out of almost six months you got help! That's not much," Aunt Arlene protests. "That's nothing. You deserve the credit, honey."

"Aunt Arlene," I say, slowly and carefully, "why don't you do me a big favor? Leave Grover alone, but go set everyone else straight."

"I certainly will!" Aunt Arlene says, and she is out of the door in a flash.

"I guess your aunt Arlene has come around concerning your pumpkin growing," Daddy says.

"I guess so." I make a funny, smart-aleck face, and we both crack up.

Chapter 38

May 2, my birthday, has come and gone, and suddenly it's the first day of summer vacation. In a few weeks Grandma and Grandpa will be arriving for their annual Ohio trip; they're coming the end of June. This time, instead of us traveling to West Virginia, Uncle Harry and Aunt Lois are coming here. They are bringing Amanda with them too, which I'm really happy about. Unfortunately, though, I will not be able to show her how to grow giant pumpkins like I said I would. There is no vine coming up through brown soil in my backyard. Just didn't feel the need to grow anything this year.

I overheard Aunt Arlene telling Daddy last week, "I'm glad she won last October, but what a relief she is over that phase! She needs to find other things to be interested in, and now she will finally have a chance."

I knew it was too good to be true. She was back to her old ways. I felt myself growing all prickly and upset. For a split second I thought about bursting into the room to give Aunt Arlene a piece of my mind. But Daddy put her in her place.

"Well, if she had to go through a phase, one that had to do with growing pumpkins wasn't all that bad, if you ask me," Daddy replied, and you could tell by his voice he was getting huffy with her.

There was a long pause, and then Aunt Arlene finally said, "I suppose you're right. You know, sometimes I think by tending to those pumpkins, she was tending to her grief. Maybe I shouldn't have given her such a hard time about it."

With those words, the prickliness that I was just

feeling toward Aunt Arlene slowly melted away.

Late afternoon yesterday, while I was out walking Arnold and Wilber, Jacob came flying down the driveway on his bike, a little trail of dust from gravel streaming behind him. He put the kickstand down, took off his helmet, and followed me, Arnold, and Wilber to the backyard. Wilber stopped to hike his leg and Jacob stopped too, staring at the weeds poking up through what used to be my pumpkin patch. I'm sure he noticed the barren patch long ago, but he finally gathered the courage to ask me about it. "Not growing one this year?"

"Nope."

"What did you do with the seeds you saved from your pumpkin, then? After you won, you told me they'd be worth their weight in gold."

I studied my dirty tennis shoe, twisting the toe into the ground, then I looked sheepishly at Jacob. "I gave them to Grover Fernhart."

"No way." Jacob appeared dumbfounded with this news.

"Yes way." I stuck my hands in my back pockets and shrugged, grinning. "And guess what? I really truly hope he wins this time."

Jacob laughed. "Actually, I hope he does, too."

There were a few moments of silence, then Jacob asked, "Want to make dirt ramps in the field for our bikes?"

"Sure."

Jacob never did ask why I stopped.

Maybe he knew I wasn't real sure myself.

What I do know, though, is that pumpkin or not, I'll always carry Mama in my heart. Daddy gave me Mama's Pumpkin Queen picture for my birthday. I have it on my bedside table, so every night Mama smiles at me from under a twinkling crown. And every night I turn off the light, snuggle into the covers, and smile back at her through the darkness.

Acknowledgments

Since half my growing-up years took place in Pickaway County, the Pumpkin Show is near and dear to my heart. Though no longer a resident, I can still be found wandering the crowded streets of Circleville every year, eating the delicious food and admiring the current crop of giant pumpkins. I've always been intrigued by the giants but never tried growing one. To be honest, I can't even grow a houseplant; I've killed off many of those. So with no green thumb to depend on, I immersed myself in research. I scoured the Internet and read several editions of Don Langevin's *How-to-Grow World Class Giant Pumpkins*. Although I've never met or spoken to Don, I am deeply indebted to him. His books were a constant companion during the writing process. For anyone interested in growing giant pumpkins, his books are an excellent place to start. I would also like to thank Dr. Robert Liggett, who not only won the pumpkin weigh-off in 2004 but broke the thousand-pound barrier at the Circleville Pumpkin Show in a big way. After all the research I had done, there were still questions that lingered, and he was kind enough to lend his time and expertise. We exchanged quite a few e-mails, and the information he provided was invaluable. If there are any errors to be found in Mildred's story, I certainly claim them as mine and mine alone; they are definitely not the result of our correspondence.

Last but not least, special thanks and much gratitude go out to my agent, Wendy Schmalz; publisher, Virginia Duncan, and editor, Martha Mihalick. Mildred not only had Aunt Arlene to contend with, but these busybodies as well! My main character is most fortunate to have had Wendy, Virginia, and Martha looking out for her in the most caring way possible. And I consider myself extremely lucky to have them as part of my life story too.